CARTER SCHOLZ

HDRAWN

Nominated for the Campbell Award
Locus Award
Nebula Award
Hugo Award

"Calvino, DeLillo, and David Foster Wallace come
to mind. . . . Scholz weaves the analytical, the literal,
the literary, the imaginary, and the emotional."
—*Boston Globe*

"Scholz's writing crackles with energy,
intelligence and dark humor."
—*Publishers Weekly*

"I doubt there's another writer in the country
who can match Scholz as a stylist."
—Karen Joy Fowler

"Extraordinarily talented."
—*Booklist*

"Not just intellectually provocative, but
emotionally rich, even saturated."
—*Washington Post Book World*

"Freakishly gifted."
—*San Francisco Chronicle*

"Serious, engrossing."
—*New York Times Book Review*

PM PRESS OUTSPOKEN AUTHORS SERIES

PM PRESS OUTSPOKEN AUTHORS SERIES

Gypsy

plus...

THIS BOOK IS A GIFT FROM THE FRIENDS OF THE ORINDA LIBRARY

THE FRIENDS OF THE ORINDA LIBRARY

Gypsy

plus

"The Nine Billion Names of God"

and

"The United States of Impunity"

and

"Bad Pennies"

and

"Gear. Food. Rocks."

Outspoken Interview

Carter Scholz

PM PRESS | 2015

"The Nine Billion Names of God" originally appeared in *Light Years and Dark: Science Fiction and Fantasy of and for Our Time*, ed. Michael Bishop (New York: Berkley Books, 1984); "Bad Pennies" originally appeared online in *Flurb: A Webzine of Astonishing Tales* no. 8 (Fall–Winter 2009), ed. Rudy Rucker, available at http://www.flurb.net/8/index8.html

Gypsy, Carter Scholz © 2015
This edition © 2015 PM Press
Series editor: Terry Bisson

ISBN: 9781629631189
Library of Congress Control Number: 2015930899

Outsides: John Yates/Stealworks.com • Insides: Jonathan Rowland

PM Press • P.O. Box 23912 • Oakland, CA 94623

10 9 8 7 6 5 4 3 2 1

Printed in the USA by the Employee Owners of Thomson-Shore in Dexter, Michigan
www.thomsonshore.com

CONTENTS

GYPSY

The living being is only a species of the dead, and a very rare species.

—Nietzsche

When a long shot is all you have, you're a fool not to take it.

—Romany saying

for Cheryl

1.

The launch of Earth's first starship went unremarked. The crew gave no interviews. No camera broadcast the hard light pulsing from its tail. To the plain eye, it might have been a common airplane.

The media battened on multiple wars and catastrophes. The Arctic Ocean was open sea. Florida was underwater. Crises and opportunities intersected.

World population was something over ten billion. No one was really counting anymore. A few billion were stateless refugees. A few billion more were indentured or imprisoned.

Oil reserves, declared as recently as 2010 to exceed a trillion barrels, proved to be an accounting gimmick, gone by 2020. More difficult and expensive sources—tar sands in Canada and Venezuela, natural gas fracking—became primary, driving up atmospheric methane and the price of fresh water.

The countries formerly known as the Third World stripped and sold their resources with more ruthless abandon than their mentors had. With the proceeds they armed themselves.

The US was no longer the global hyperpower, but it went on behaving as if. Generations of outspending the rest of the world combined had made this its habit and brand: arms merchant to expedient allies, former and future foes alike, starting or provoking conflicts more or less at need, its constant need being, as always, resources. Its waning might was built on a memory of those vast native reserves it had long since expropriated and depleted, and a sense of entitlement to more. These overseas conflicts were problematic and carried wildly unintended consequences. As the president of Venezuela put it just days before his assassination, "It's dangerous to go to war against your own asshole."

The starship traveled out of our solar system at a steep angle to the ecliptic plane. It would pass no planets. It was soon gone. Going South.

SOPHIE (2043)

Trying to rise up out of the cold sinking back into a dream of rising up out of the. Stop, stop it now. Shivering. So dark. So thirsty. Momma? Help me?

• • •

Her parents were wealthy. They had investments, a great home, they sent her to the best schools. They told her how privileged she was. She'd always assumed this meant she would be okay forever. She was going to be a poet.

It was breathtaking how quickly it went away, all that okay. Her dad's job, the investments, the college tuition, the house. In two years, like so many others they were penniless and living in their car. She left unfinished her thesis on Louis Zukofsky's last book, 80 Flowers. *She changed her major to Information Science, slept with a loan officer, finished grad school half a million in debt, and immediately took the best-paying job she could find, at Xocket Defense Systems. Librarian. She hadn't known that defense contractors hired librarians. They were pretty much the only ones who did anymore. Her student loan was adjustable rate—the only kind offered. As long as the rate didn't go up, she could just about get by on her salary. Best case, she'd have it paid off in thirty years. Then the rate doubled. She lost her apartment. XDS had huge dorms for employees who couldn't afford their own living space. Over half their workforce lived there. It was indentured servitude.*

Yet she was lucky, lucky. If she'd been a couple of years younger she wouldn't have finished school at all. She'd be fighting in Burma or Venezuela or Kazakhstan.

At XDS she tended the library's firewalls, maintained and documented software, catalogued projects, fielded service calls from personnel who needed this or that right now, or had forgotten a password, or locked themselves out of their own account. She learned Unix, wrote cron scripts and daemons and Perl routines. There was a satisfaction in keeping it all straight. She was a serf, but they needed her and they knew it, and that knowledge sustained in her a hard small sense of freedom. She thought of Zukofsky, teaching for twenty years at Brooklyn Polytech. It was almost a kind of poetry, the vocabulary of code.

• • •

Chirping. Birds? Were there still birds?

No. Tinnitus. Her ears ached for sound in this profound silence. Created their own.

• • •

She was a California girl, an athlete, a hiker, a climber. She'd been all over the Sierra Nevada, had summited four 14,000-footers by the time she was sixteen. She loved the backcountry. Loved its stark beauty, solitude, the life that survived in its harshness: the pikas, the marmots, the mountain chickadees, the heather and whitebark pine and polemonium.

After joining XDS, it became hard for her to get to the mountains. Then it became impossible. In 2035 the Keep Wilderness Wild Act shut the public out of the national parks, the national forests, the BLM lands. The high country above timberline was surveilled by satellites and drones, and it was said that mining and fracking operators would shoot intruders on sight, and that in the remotest areas, like the Enchanted Gorge and the Muro Blanco, lived small nomadic bands of malcontents. She knew enough about the drones and satellites to doubt it; no one on Earth could stay hidden anywhere for more than a day.

The backcountry she mourned was all Earth to her. To lose it was to lose all Earth. And to harden something final inside her.

One day Roger Fry came to her attention—perhaps it was the other way round—poking in her stacks where he didn't belong. That was odd; the login and password had been validated, the clearance was the highest, there was no place in the stacks prohibited to this user; yet her alarms had tripped. By the time she put packet sniffers on it he was gone. In her e-mail was an invitation to visit a website called Gypsy.

When she logged in, she understood at once. It thrilled her and frightened her. They were going to leave the planet. It was insane. Yet she felt the powerful seduction of it. How starkly its plain insanity exposed the greater consensus insanity the planet was now living. That there was an alternative—!

• • •

She sat up on the slab. Slowly unwrapped the mylar bodysuit, disconnected one by one its drips and derms and stents and catheters and waldos and sensors. Let it drift crinkling to the floor.

Her breathing was shallow and ragged. Every few minutes she gasped for air and her pulse raced. The temperature had been raised to 20°C as she came to, but still she shivered. Her body smelled a way it had never smelled before. Like vinegar and nail polish. It looked pale and flabby, but familiar. After she'd gathered strength, she reached under the slab, found a sweatshirt and sweatpants, and pulled them on. There was also a bottle of water. She drank it all.

The space was small and dark and utterly silent. No ports, no windows. Here and there, on flat black walls, glowed a few pods of LEDs. She braced her hands against the slab and stood up, swaying. Even in the slight gravity her heart pounded. The ceiling curved gently away a handsbreadth above her head, and the floor curved gently upward. Unseen beyond the ceiling was the center of the ship, the hole of the donut, and beyond that the other half of the slowly spinning torus. Twice a minute it rotated, creating a centripetal gravity of one tenth g. Any slower would be too weak to be helpful. Any faster, gravity would differ at the head and the feet enough to cause vertigo. Under her was the outer ring of the water tank, then panels of aerogel sandwiched within sheets of hydrogenous carbon-composite, then a surrounding jacket of liquid hydrogen tanks, and then interstellar space.

What had happened? Why was she awake?

• • •

Look, over seventy plus years, systems will fail. We can't rely on auto-repair. With a crew of twenty, we could wake one person every few years to perform maintenance.

And put them back under? Hibernation is dicey enough without trying to do it twice.

Yes, it's a risk. What's the alternative?

What about failsafes? No one gets wakened unless a system is critical. Then we wake a specialist. A steward.

That could work.

• • •

She walked the short distance to the ship's console and sat. It would have been grandiose to call it a bridge. It was a small desk bolted to the floor. It held a couple of monitors, a keyboard, some pads. It was like the light and sound booth of a community theater.

She wished she could turn on more lights. There were no more. Their energy budget was too tight. They had a fission reactor onboard but it wasn't running. It was to fire the nuclear rocket at their arrival. It wouldn't last seventy-two years if they used it for power during their cruise.

Not far from her—nothing on the ship was far from her—were some fifty kilograms of plutonium pellets—not the Pu-239 of fission bombs, but the more energetic Pu-238. The missing neutron cut the isotope's half-life from twenty-five thousand years to eighty-eight years and made it proportionately more radioactive. That alpha radiation was contained by iridium cladding and a casing of graphite, but the pellets still gave off heat, many kilowatts' worth. Most of that heat warmed the ship's interior to its normal temperature of 4°C. Enough of it was channeled outward to keep the surrounding water liquid in its jacket, and the outer tanks of hydrogen at 14 Kelvins, slush, maximally dense. The rest of the heat ran a Stirling engine to generate electricity.

First she read through the protocols, which she had written: *Stewards' logs to be read by each wakened steward. Kept in the computers, with redundant backups, but also kept by hand, ink* on paper, in case of system failures, a last-chance critical backup. And because there is something restorative about writing by hand.

There were no stewards' logs. She was the first to be wakened.

They were only two years out. Barely into the Oort cloud. She felt let down. What had gone wrong so soon?

All at once she was ravenous. She stood, and the gravity differential hit her. She steadied herself against the desk, then took two steps to the storage bay. Three quarters of the ship was storage. What they would need at the other end. What Roger called pop-up civilization. She only had to go a step inside to find a box of MREs. She took three, and put one into the microwave. The smell of it warming made her mouth water and her stomach heave. Her whole body trembled as she ate. Immediately she put a second into the microwave. As she waited for it, she fell asleep.

● ● ●

She saw Roger, what must have happened to him after that terrible morning when they received his message: Go. Go now. Go at once.

He was wearing an orange jumpsuit, shackled to a metal table.

How did you think you could get away with it, Fry?

I did get away with it. They've gone.

But we've got you.

That doesn't matter. I was never meant to be aboard.

Where are they going?

Alpha Centauri. (He would pronounce it with the hard K.)

That's impossible.

Very likely. But that's where they're going.
Why?
It's less impossible than here.

•••

When she opened her eyes, her second meal had cooled, but she didn't want it. Her disused bowels protested. She went to the toilet and strained but voided only a trickle of urine. Feeling ill, she hunched in the dark, small space, shivering, sweat from her armpits running down her ribs. The smell of her urine mixed with the toilet's chemicals and the sweetly acrid odor of her long fast.

pleine de l'âcre odeur des temps, poudreuse et noire
full of the acrid smell of time, dusty and black

Baudelaire. Another world. With wonder she felt it present itself. Consciousness was a mystery. She stared into the darkness, fell asleep again on the pot.

•••

Again she saw Roger shackled to the metal table. A door opened and he looked up.

We've decided.

He waited.

Your ship, your crew, your people—they don't exist. No one will ever know about them.

Roger was silent.

The ones remaining here, the ones who helped you—you're thinking we can't keep them all quiet. We can. We're into your private keys. We know everyone who was involved. We'll round them up. The number's small enough. After all your work, Roger, all their years of effort, there will be nothing but a few pathetic rumors and conspiracy theories. All those good people who helped you will be disappeared forever. Like you. How does that make you feel?

    They knew the risks. For them it was already over. Like me.

    Over? Oh, Roger. We can make "over" last a long time.

    Still, we did it. They did it. They know that.

    You're not hearing me, Roger. I said we've changed that.

    The ship is out there.

    No. I said it's not. Repeat after me. Say it's not, Roger.

• • •

BUFFER OVERFLOW. So that was it. Their datastream was not being received. Sophie had done much of the information theory design work. An energy-efficient system approaching Shannon's limit for channel capacity. Even from Alpha C it would be only ten joules per bit.

The instruments collected data. Magnetometer, spectrometers, plasma analyzer, cosmic-ray telescope, Cerenkov detector, et cetera. Data was queued in a transmit buffer and sent out more or less continuously at a low bit rate. The protocol was designed to be robust against interference, dropped packets, interstellar scintillation, and the long latencies imposed by their great distance and the speed of light.

• • •

They'd debated even whether to carry communications.

What's the point? We're turning our backs on them.

Roger was insistent: Are we scientists? This is an unprecedented chance to collect data in the heliopause, the Oort cloud, the interstellar medium, the Alpha system itself. Astrometry from Alpha, reliable distances to every star in our galaxy—that alone is huge.

Sending back data broadcasts our location.

So? How hard is it to follow a nuclear plasma trail to the nearest star? Anyway, they'd need a ship to follow. We have the only one.

You say the Earth situation is terminal. Who's going to receive this data?

Anybody. Everybody.

• • •

So: Shackleton Crater. It was a major comm link anyway, and its site at the south pole of the Moon assured low ambient noise and permanent line of sight to the ship. They had a Gypsy there—one of their tribe—to receive their data.

The datastream was broken up into packets, to better weather the long trip home. Whenever Shackleton received a packet, it responded with an acknowledgement, to confirm reception. When the ship received that ACK signal—at their present distance, that would be about two months after a packet was transmitted—the confirmed packet was removed from the transmit queue to make room for new data. Otherwise the packet went back to the end of the queue, to be retransmitted later. Packets were time-stamped, so they could be reassembled into a consecutive datastream no matter in what order they were received.

But no ACK signals had been received for over a year. The buffer was full. That's why she was awake.

They'd known the Shackleton link could be broken, even though it had a plausible cover story of looking for SETI transmissions from Alpha C. But other Gypsies on Earth should also be receiving. Someone should be acknowledging. A year of silence!

Going back through computer logs, she found there'd been an impact. Eight months ago something had hit the ship. Why hadn't that wakened a steward?

It had been large enough to get through the forward electromagnetic shield. The shield deflected small particles which, over decades, would erode their hull. The damage had been instantaneous. Repair geckos responded in the first minutes. Since it took most of a day to rouse a steward, there would have been no point.

Maybe the impact hit the antenna array. She checked and adjusted alignment to the Sun. They were okay. She took a routine spectrograph and measured the Doppler shift.

0.056 c.

No. Their velocity should be 0.067 c.

Twelve years. It added twelve years to their cruising time.

She studied the ship's logs as that sank in. The fusion engine had burned its last over a year ago, then was jettisoned to spare mass.

Why hadn't a steward awakened before her? The computer hadn't logged any problems. Engine function read as normal; the sleds that held the fuel had been emptied one by one and discarded as the fuel had been burned—all as planned. So, absent other problems, the lower velocity alone hadn't triggered an alert. Stupid!

Think. They'd begun to lag only in the last months of burn. Some ignitions must have failed or underperformed. It was probably antiproton decay in the triggers. Nothing could have corrected that. Good thinking, nice fail.

Twelve years.

It angered her. The impact and the low velocity directly threatened their survival, and no alarms went off. But loss of comms, *that* set off alarms, that was important to Roger. Who was never meant to be on board. *He's turned his back on humanity, but he still wants them to hear all about it. And to hell with us.*

When her fear receded, she was calmer. If Roger still believed in anything redeemable about humankind, it was the scientific impulse. Of course it was primary to him that this ship do science, and send data. This was her job.

• • •

Why Alpha C? Why so impossibly far?

Why not the Moon? The US was there: the base at Shackleton, with a ten-thousand-acre solar power plant, a deuterium mine in the lunar ice, and a twenty-gigawatt particle beam. The Chinese were on the far side, mining helium-3 from the regolith.

Why not Mars? China was there. A one-way mission had been sent in 2025. The crew might not have survived—that was classified—but the robotics had. The planet was reachable and therefore dangerous.

Jupiter? There were rumors that the US was there as well, maybe the Chinese too, robots anyway, staking a claim to all that helium. Roger didn't put much credence in the rumors, but they might be true.

Why not wait it out at a Lagrange point? Roger thought there was nothing to wait for. The situation was terminal. As things spiraled down the maelstrom, anyplace cislunar would be at risk. Sooner or later any ship out there would be detected and destroyed. Or it might last only because civilization was shattered, with the survivors in some pit plotting to pummel the shards.

It was Alpha C because Roger Fry was a fanatic who believed that only an exit from the solar system offered humanity any hope of escaping what it had become.

She thought of Sergei, saying in his bad accent and absent grammar, which he exaggerated for effect: This is shit. You say me Alpha See is best? Absolute impossible. Is double star, no planet in habitable orbit—yes yes, whatever, minima maxima, zone of hopeful bullshit. Ghost Planet Hope. You shoot load there?

How long they had argued over this—their destination.

Gliese 581.

Impossible.

Roger, it's a rocky planet with liquid water.

That's three mistakes in one sentence. Something is orbiting the star, with a period of thirteen days and a mass of two Earths and some spectral lines. Rocky, water, liquid, that's all surmise. What's for sure is it's twenty light-years away. Plus, the star is a flare star. It's disqualified twice before we even get to the hope-it's-a-planet part.

You don't know it's a flare star! There are no observations!

In the absence of observations, we assume it behaves like other observed stars of its class. It flares.

You have this agenda for Alpha C. You've invented these criteria to shoot down every other candidate!

The criteria are transparent. We've agreed to them. Number one: twelve light-years is our outer limit. Right there we're down to twenty-four stars. For reasons of luminosity and stability we prefer a nonvariable G- or K-class star. Now we're down to five. Alpha Centauri, Epsilon Eridani, 61 Cygni, Epsilon Indi, and Tau Ceti make the cut. Alpha is half the distance of the next nearest.

Bullshit, Roger. You have bug up ass for your Alpha See. Why not disqualify as double, heh? Why this not shoot-down criteria?

Because we have modeled it, and we know planet formation is possible in this system, and we have direct evidence of planets in other double systems. And because—I know.

They ended with Alpha because it was closest. Epsilon Eridani had planets for sure, but they were better off with a closer Ghost Planet Hope than a sure thing so far they couldn't reach it. Cosmic rays would degrade the electronics, the ship, their very cells. Every year in space brought them closer to some component's MTBF: mean time between failures.

• • •

Well, they'd known they might lose Shackleton. It was even likely. Just not so soon.

She'd been pushing away the possibility that things had gone so badly on Earth that no one was left to reply.

• • •

She remembered walking on a fire road after a conference in Berkeley—the Bay dappled sapphire and russet, thick white marine layer pushing in over the Golden Gate Bridge—talking to Roger about Fermi's Paradox. If the universe harbors life, intelligence, why haven't we seen evidence of it? Why are we alone? Roger favored what he called the Mean Time Between Failures argument. Technological civilizations simply fail, just as the components that make up their technology fail, sooner or later, for reasons as individually insignificant as they are inexorable, and final. Complex systems, after a point, tend away from robustness.

● ● ●

Okay. Any receivers on Earth will have to find their new signal. It was going to be like SETI in reverse: she had to make the new signal maximally detectable. She could do that. She could retune the frequency to better penetrate Earth's atmosphere. Reprogram the PLLs and antenna array, use orthogonal FSK modulation across the K- and X-bands. Increase the buffer size. And hope for the best.

Eighty-four years to go. My God, they were barely out the front door. My God, it was lonely out here.

The mission plan had been seventy-two years, with a predicted systems-failure rate of under 20 percent. The Weibull curve climbed steeply after that. At eighty-four years, systems-failure rate was over 50 percent.

What could be done to speed them? The nuclear rocket and its fuel were for deceleration and navigation at the far end. To use it here would add—she calculated—a total of 0.0002 c to their current speed. Saving them all of three months. And leaving them no means of planetfall.

They had nothing. Their cruise velocity was unalterable.

All right, that's that, so find a line. Commit to it and move.

Cruise at this speed for longer, decelerate later and harder. That could save a few years. They'd have to run more current through the magsail, increase its drag, push its specs.

Enter the Alpha C system faster than planned, slow down harder once within it. She didn't know how to calculate those maneuvers, but someone else would.

Her brain was racing now, wouldn't let her sleep. She'd been up for three days. These were not her decisions to make, but she was the only one who could.

She wrote up detailed logs with the various options and calculations she'd made. At last there was no more for her to do. But a sort of nostalgia came over her. She wanted, absurdly, to check her e-mail. Really, just to hear some voice not her own.

Nothing broadcast from Earth reached this far except for the ACK signals beamed directly to them from Shackleton. Shackleton was also an IPN node, connecting space assets to the internet. For cover, the ACK signals it sent to *Gypsy* were piggybacked on internet packets. And those had all been stored by the computer.

So in her homesick curiosity, she called them out of memory, and dissected some packets that had been saved from up to a year ago. Examined their broken and scrambled content like a torn, discarded newspaper for anything they might tell her of the planet she'd never see again.

•••

`M.3,S+SDS#0U4:&ES(&%R=&EC;&4@:7,@8V]P>7`

Warmer than usual regime actively amplifies tundra thaw. Drought melt permafrost thermokarsts methane burn wildfire giants 800 ppm. Capture hot atmospheric ridge NOAA front-running collapse sublime asymmetric artificial trade resource loss.

`M1HE9LXO6FXQLKL86KWQLUN;AXEW)1VZ!"NHS;S`

Weapon tensions under Islamic media policy rebels arsenals strategic counterinsurgency and to prevent Federal war law operational artillery air component to mine mountain strongholds photorecce altitudes HQ backbone Su-35 SAMs part with high maneuverability bombardments of casualty casuistry

`M87EL;W(@)B!&<F%N8VES+"Q.3P($9R;W-T#5)O`

Hurriedly autoimmune decay derivative modern thaws in dawn's pregnant grave shares in disgust of high frequency trading wet cities territorial earthquake poison Bayes the chairs are empty incentives to disorder without borders. Pneumonia again antibiotic resistance travels the globe with ease.

`M7V35EX-SR'KP8G49:YZSR/BBJWS82<9NS(!1W^`

Knowing perpendicular sex dating in Knob Lick Missouri stateroom Sweeney atilt with cheerfully synodic weeny or restorative ministration. Glintingly aweigh triacetate hopefully occasionally sizeable interrogation nauseate. Descriptive mozzarella cosmos truly and contumacious portability.

`M4F]N9F5L9'0-26YT97)N871I;VYA;"!0;VQI8W`

Titter supine teratologys aim appoint to plaintive technocrat. Mankind is inwardly endocrine and afar romanic spaceflight. Mesial corinths archidiaconal or lyric satirical turtle

demurral. Calorific fitment marry after sappy are inscribed upto pillwort. Idem monatomic are processed longways
`M#0U#;W!Y<FEG:'0@,3DY,R!487EL;W(@)B!&<F`

archive tittie blowjob hair fetish SEX FREE PICS RUSSIAN hardcore incest stories animate porn wankers benedict paris car motorcycle cop fetish sex toys caesar milfhunters when im found this pokemon porn gallery fisting Here Is Links to great her lesbiands Sites
`M0UE"15)705(@25,@0T]-24Y'(0T-2F]H;B!!<G`

• • •

Lost, distant, desolate. The world she'd left forever, speaking its poison poetry of ruin and catastrophe and longing. Told her nothing she didn't already know about the corrupt destiny and thwarted feeling that had drawn humankind into the maelstrom *Gypsy* had escaped. She stood and walked furiously the meager length of the curved corridor, stopping at each slab, regarding the sleeping forms of her crewmates, naked in translucent bodysuits, young and fit, yet broken, like her, in ways that had made this extremity feel to them all the only chance.

• • •

They gathered together for the first time on the ship after receiving Roger's signal.

We'll be fine. Not even Roger knows where the ship is. They won't be able to find us before we're gone.

It was her first time in space. From the shuttle, the ship appeared a formless clutter: layers of bomb sleds, each bearing thousands of microfusion devices, under and around them a jacket of hydrogen tanks, shields, conduits, antennas. Two white-suited figures crawled over this maze. A hijacked hydrogen depot was offloading its cargo.

Five were already aboard, retrofitting. Everything not needed for deep space had been jettisoned. Everything lacking was brought and secured. Shuttles that were supposed to be elsewhere came and went on encrypted itineraries.

One shuttle didn't make it. They never learned why. So they were down to sixteen crew.

The ship wasn't meant to hold so many active people. The crew area was less than a quarter of the torus, a single room narrowed to less than ten feet by the hibernation slabs lining each long wall. Dim even with all the LED bays on.

Darius opened champagne. Contraband: no one knew how alcohol might interact with the hibernation drugs.

To Andrew and Chung-Pei and Hari and Maryam. They're with us in spirit.

Some time later the first bomb went off. The ship trembled but didn't move. Another blast. Then another. Grudgingly the great mass budged. Like a car departing a curb, no faster at first. Fuel mass went from it and kinetic energy into it. Kinesis was gradual but unceasing. In its first few minutes it advanced less than a kilometer. In its first hour it moved two thousand kilometers. In its first day, a million kilometers. After a year, when the last bomb was expended, it would be some two thousand astronomical units from the Earth, and Gypsy *would coast on at her fixed speed for decades, a dark, silent, near-dead thing.*

• • •

As Sophie prepared to return to hibernation, she took stock. She walked the short interior of the quarter-torus. Less than twenty paces end to end. The black walls, the dim LED pods, the slabs of her crewmates.

Never to see her beloved mountains again. Her dear sawtooth Sierra. She thought of the blue sky, and remembered a hunk of stuff she'd seen on Roger's desk, some odd kind of rock. It was about five inches long. You could see through it. Its edges were blurry. Against a dark background it had a bluish tinge. She took it in her hand and it was nearly weightless.

What is this?

Silica aerogel. The best insulator in the world.

Why is it blue?

Rayleigh scattering.

She knew what that meant: why the sky is blue. Billions of particles in the air scatter sunlight, shorter wavelengths scatter most, so those suffuse the sky. The shortest we can see is blue. But that was an ocean of air around the planet and this was a small rock.

You're joking.

No, it's true. There are billions of internal surfaces in that piece.

It's like a piece of sky.

Yes, it is.

It was all around her now, that stuff—in the walls of the ship, keeping out the cold of space—allowing her to imagine a poetry of sky where none was.

● ● ●

And that was it. She'd been awake for five days. She'd fixed the datastream back to Earth. She'd written her logs. She'd reprogrammed the magsail deployment for seventy years from now, at increased current, in the event that no other steward was wakened in the meantime. She'd purged her bowels and injected the hibernation cocktail. She was back in the bodysuit, life supports connected. As she went under, she wondered why.

2.

They departed a day short of Roger Fry's fortieth birthday. Born September 11, 2001, he was hired to a national weapons laboratory straight out of Caltech. He never did finish his doctorate. Within a year at the Lab he had designed the first breakeven fusion reaction. It had long been known that a very small amount of antimatter could trigger a burn wave in thermonuclear fuel. Roger solved how. He was twenty-four.

Soon there were net energy gains. That's when the bomb people came in. In truth, their interest was why he was hired in the first place. Roger knew this and didn't care. Once fusion became a going concern, it would mean unlimited clean energy. It would change the world. Bombs would have no purpose.

But it was a long haul to a commercial fusion reactor. Meanwhile, bombs were easier.

The first bombs were shaped-charge antiproton-triggered fusion bunker busters. The smallest was a kiloton-yield bomb, powerful enough to level forty or fifty city blocks; it used just a hundred grams of lithium deuteride, and less than a microgram of antimatter. It was easy to manufacture and transport and deploy. It created little radiation or electromagnetic pulse. Tens of thousands, then hundreds of thousands, were fabricated in orbit and moved to drop platforms called sleds. Because the minimum individual yields were within the range of conventional explosives, no nuclear treaties were violated.

Putting them in orbit did violate the Outer Space Treaty, so at first they were more politely called the Orbital Asteroid Defense Network. But when a large asteroid passed through cislunar space a few years later—with no warning, no alert, no response at all—the pretense was dropped, and the system came under the command of the US Instant Global Strike Initiative.

More and more money went into antimatter production. There were a dozen factories worldwide that produced about a gram, all told, of antiprotons a year. Some went into the first fusion power plants, which themselves produced more antiprotons. Most went into bomb triggers. There they were held in traps, isolated from normal matter—but that worked only so long. They decayed, like tritium in the older nuclear weapons, but much faster; some traps could store milligrams of antiprotons for many months at a time, and they were improving; still, bomb triggers had to be replaced often.

As a defence system it was insane, but hugely profitable. Then came the problem of where to park the profits, since there were no stable markets anywhere. The economic system most rewarded those whose created and surfed instabilities and could externalize their risks, which created greater instabilities.

Year after year Roger worked and waited, and the number of bombs grew, as did the number of countries deploying them, and the global resource wars intensified, and his fusion utopia failed to arrive. When the first commercial plants did start operating, it made no difference. Everything went on as before. Those who had the power to change things had no reason to; things had worked out pretty well for them so far.

Atmospheric CO_2 shot past 600 parts per million. The methane burden was now measured in parts per million, not parts per billon. No one outside the classified world knew the exact numbers, but the effects were everywhere. The West Antarctic ice shelf collapsed. Sea level rose three meters.

Some time in there, Roger Fry gave up on Earth.

But not on humanity, not entirely. Something in the complex process of civilization had forced it into this place from which it now had no exit. He didn't see this as an inevitable result of the process, but it had happened. There might have been a time when the situation was reversible. If certain decisions had been made. If resources had been treated as a commons. Back when the population of the planet was two or three billion, when there was still enough to go around, enough time to alter course, enough leisure to think things through. But it hadn't gone that way. He didn't much care why. The question was what to do now.

FANG TIR EOGHAIN (2081)

The ancestor of all mammals must have been a hibernator. Body temperature falls as much as 15 Kelvins. A bear's heartbeat goes down to five per minute. Blood pressure drops to thirty mil-limeters. In humans, these conditions would be fatal.

Relatively few genes are involved in torpor. We have located the critical ones. And we have found the protein complexes they uptake and produce. Monophosphates mostly.

Yes, I know, induced hypothermia is not torpor. But this state has the signatures of torpor. For example, there is a surfeit of MCT1 which transports ketones to the brain during fasting.

Ketosis, that's true, we are in a sense poisoning the subject in order to achieve this state. Some ischemia and refusion damage results, but less than anticipated. Doing it more than a couple of times is sure to be fatal. But for our purposes, maybe it gets the job done.

Anyway it had better; we have nothing else.

• • •

Her da was screaming at her to get up. He wasn't truly her father; her father had gone to the stars. That was a story she'd made up long ago. It was better than the truth.

Her thick brown legs touched the floor. Not so thick and brown as she remembered. Weak, pale, withered. She tried to stand and fell back. Try harder, cow. She fell asleep.

• • •

She'd tried so hard for so long. She'd been accepted early at university. Then her parents went afoul of the system. One day she came home to a bare apartment. All are zhonghua minzu, *but it was a bad time for certain ethnics in China.*

She lost her place at university. She was shunted to a polytechnic secondary in Guangzhou, where she lived with her aunt and uncle in a small apartment. It wasn't science; it was job training in technology services. One day she overheard the uncle on the phone, bragging: he had turned her parents in, collected a bounty and a stipend.

She was not yet fifteen. It was still possible, then, to be adopted out of country. Covertly, she set about it. Caitlin Tyrone was the person who helped her from afar.

They'd met online, in a science chatroom. Ireland needed scientists. She didn't know or care where that was; she'd have gone to Hell. It took almost a year to arrange it, the adoption. It took all Fang's diligence, all her cunning, all her need, all her cold hate, to keep it from her uncle, to acquire the paperwork, to forge his signature, to sequester money, and finally on the last morning to sneak out of the apartment before dawn.

She flew from Guangzhao to Beijing to Frankfurt to Dublin, too nervous to sleep. Each time she had to stop in an airport and wait for the next flight, sometimes for hours, she feared arrest. In her sleepless imagination, the waiting lounges turned into detention centers. Then she was on the last flight. The stars faded and the sun rose over the Atlantic, and there was Ireland. O! the green of it. And her new mother Caitlin was there to greet her, grab her, look into her eyes. Goodbye forever to the wounded past.

She had a scholarship at Trinity College, in biochemistry. She already knew English, but during her first year she studied phonology and orthography and grammar, to try to map, linguistically, how far she'd traveled. It wasn't so far. The human vocal apparatus is everywhere the same. So is the brain, constructing the grammar that drives the voice box. Most of her native phonemes had Irish or

English equivalents, near enough. But the sounds she made of hers were not quite correct, so she worked daily to refine them.

O is where she often came to rest. The exclamative particle, the sound of that moment when the senses surprise the body, same in Ireland as in China—same body, same senses, same sound. Yet a human universe of shadings. The English O was one thing; Mandarin didn't quite have it; Cantonese was closer; but everywhere the sound slid around depending on locality, on country, even on county: monophthong to diphthong, the tongue wandering in the mouth, seeking to settle. When she felt lost in the night, which was often, she sought for that O, round and solid and vast and various and homey as the planet beneath her, holding her with its gravity. Moving her tongue in her mouth as she lay in bed waiting for sleep.

Biochemistry wasn't so distant, in her mind, from language. She saw it all as signaling. DNA wasn't "information," data held statically in helices, it was activity, transaction.

She insisted on her new hybrid name, the whole long Gaelic mess of it—it was Caitlin's surname—as a reminder of the contingency of belonging, of culture and language, of identity itself. Her solid legs had landed on solid ground, or solid enough to support her.

• • •

Carefully, arduously, one connector at a time, she unplugged herself from the bodysuit, then sat up on the slab. Too quickly. She dizzied and pitched forward.

Get up, you cow. The da again. Dream trash. As if she couldn't. She'd show him. She gave all her muscles a great heave.

And woke shivering on the carbon deckplates. Held weakly down by the thin false gravity. It was no embracing O, just a trickle of mockery. *You have to do this,* she told her will.

She could small acetone on her breath. Glycogen used up, body starts to burn fat, produces ketones. Ketoacidosis. She should check ketone levels in the others.

● ● ●

Roger came into Fang's life by way of Caitlin. Years before, Caitlin had studied physics at Trinity. Roger had read her papers. They were brilliant. He'd come to teach a seminar, and he had the idea of recruiting her to the Lab. But science is bound at the hip to its application, and turbulence occurs at that interface where theory meets practice, knowledge meets performance. Where the beauty of the means goes to die in the instrumentality of the ends.

Roger found to his dismay that Caitlin couldn't manage even the sandbox politics of grad school. She'd been aced out of the best advisors and was unable to see that her science career was already in a death spiral. She'd never make it on her own at the Lab, or in a corp. He could intervene to some degree, but he was reluctant; he saw a better way.

Already Caitlin was on U, a Merck pharmaceutical widely prescribed for a new category in DSM-6: "social interoperability disorder." U for eudaimoniazine. Roger had tried it briefly himself. In his opinion, half the planet fit the diagnostic criteria, which was excellent business for Merck but said more about planetary social conditions than about the individuals who suffered under them.

U was supposed to increase compassion for others, to make other people seem more real. But Caitlin was already too empathic for her own good, too ready to yield her place to others, and the U merely blissed her out, put her in a zone of self-abnegation. Perhaps that's why it was a popular street drug; when some governments tried to ban it, Merck sued them under global trade agreements, for loss of expected future profits.

Caitlin ended up sidelined in the Trinity library, where she met and married James, an older charming sociopath with terrific interoperability. Meanwhile, Roger kept tabs on her from afar. He hacked James's medical records and noted that James was infertile.

• • •

It took Fang several hours to come to herself. She tried not to worry, this was to be expected. Her body had gone through a serious near-death trauma. She felt weak, nauseous, and her head throbbed, but she was alive. That she was sitting here sipping warm tea was a triumph, for her body and for her science. She still felt a little stunned, a little distant from that success. So many things could have gone wrong: hibernation was only the half of it; like every other problem they'd faced, it came with its own set of ancillaries. On which she'd worked.

In addition to her highly classified DARPA work on hibernation, Fang had published these papers in the *Journal of Gravitational Physiology*: Serum leptin level is a regulator of bone mass (2033); Inhibition of osteopenia by low magnitude, high frequency mechanical stimuli (2035); The transcription factor NF-kappaB is a key intracellular signal transducer in disuse atrophy (2036); IGF-I stimulates muscle growth by suppressing protein breakdown and expression of atrophy-related ubiquitin ligases, atrogin-1 and MuRF1 (2037); and PGC-1alpha protects skeletal muscle from atrophy by suppressing FoxO3 action and atrophy-specific gene transcription (2039).

When she felt able, she checked on the others. Each sleeper bore implanted and dermal sensors—for core and skin temperature, EKG, EEG, pulse, blood pressure and flow, plasma ions, plasma metabolites, clotting function, respiratory rate and depth, gas analysis and flow, urine production, EMG, tremor, body composition. Near-infrared spectrometry measured haematocrit, blood glucose, tissue O_2 and pH. Muscles were stimulated electrically and mechanically to counteract atrophy. The slabs tipped thirty degrees up or down and rotated the body from supine to prone in order to provide mechanical loading from hypogravity in all directions. Exoskeletal waldos at the joints, and the soles and fingers, provided periodic range-of-motion stimulus. A range of pharmacological and genetic interventions further regulated bone and muscle regeneration.

Also, twitching was important. If you didn't twitch you wouldn't wake. It was a kind of mooring to the present.

Did they dream? EEGs showed periodic variation but were so unlike normal EEGs that it was hard to say. You couldn't very well wake someone to ask, as the first sleep researchers had done.

All looked well on the monitor, except for number fourteen. Reza. Blood pressure almost nonexistent. She got to her feet and walked down the row of slabs to have a look at Reza.

A pursed grayish face sagging on its skull. Maybe a touch of life was visible, some purple in the gray, blood still coursing. Or maybe not.

Speckling the gray skin was a web of small white dots, each the size of a pencil eraser or smaller. They were circular but not perfectly so, margins blurred. Looked like a fungus.

She went back and touched the screen for records. This steward was long overdue for rousing. The machine had started the warming cycle three times. Each time he hadn't come out of torpor, so the machine had shut down the cycle, stabilized him, and tried again. After three failures, it had moved down the list to the next steward. Her.

She touched a few levels deeper. Not enough fat on this guy. Raising the temperature without rousing would simply bring on ischemia and perfusion. That's why the machine gave up. It was a delicate balance, to keep the metabolism burning fat instead of carbohydrates, without burning too much of the body's stores. Humans couldn't bulk up on fat in advance the way natural hibernators could. But she thought she'd solved that with the nutrient derms.

It was the fortieth year of the voyage. They were two light-years from home. Not quite halfway. If hibernation was failing now, they had a serious problem.

Was the fungus a result or a cause? Was it a fungus? She wanted to open the bodysuit and run tests, but any contagion had to be contained.

They'd discussed possible failure modes. Gene activity in bacteria increased in low gravity; they evolved more rapidly. In the presence of a host they became more virulent. Radiation caused mutations. But ultraviolet light scoured the suits every day and should have killed bacteria and fungus alike. Logs showed that the UV was functioning. It wasn't enough.

•••

James—the da, as he insisted Fang call him—had black hair and blue eyes that twinkled like ice when he smiled. At first he was mere background to her; he'd stumble in late from the pub to find Caitlin and Fang talking. Ah, the Addams sisters, he'd say, nodding sagely. Fang never understood what he meant by it. For all his geniality, he kept her at a distance, treated her like a houseguest.

Caitlin was more like an older sister than a mother; she was only twelve years older. It was fun to talk science with her, and it was helpful. She was quick to understand the details of Fang's field, and this dexterity spurred Fang in her own understanding and confidence.

After a couple of years, James grew more sullen, resentful, almost abusive. He dropped the suave act. He found fault with Fang's appearance, her habits, her character. The guest had overstayed her welcome. He was jealous.

She couldn't figure out why a woman as good and as smart as Caitlin stayed on with him. Maybe something damaged in Caitlin was called by a like damage in James. Caitlin had lost her father while a girl, as had Fang. When Fang looked at James through Caitlin's eyes, she could see in him the ruins of something strong and attractive and paternal. But that thing was no longer alive. Only Caitlin's need for it lived, and that need became a reproach to James, who had lost the ability to meet it, and who fled from it.

The further James fled into drink, the more Caitlin retreated into her U, into a quiescence where things could feel whole. All the while, James felt Fang's eyes on him, evaluating him, seeing him as he was. He saw she wasn't buying him. Nothing disturbed him more than having his act fail. And he saw that Caitlin was alive and present only with Fang. They clung to one another, and were moving away from him.

James was truly good to me, before you knew him.

On U, everyone seems good to you.

No, long before that. When I failed my orals he was a great support.

You were vulnerable. He fed on your need.

You don't know, Fang. I was lost. He helped me, he held on to me when I needed it. Then I had you.

She thought not. She thought James had learned to enjoy preying on the vulnerable. And Caitlin was too willing to ignore this, to go along with it. As Fang finished her years at Trinity, she agonized over how she must deal with this trouble. It was then that an offer arrived from Roger's lab.

Come with me to America.

Oh, Fang. I can't. What about James? What would he do there?

It was James's pretense that he was still whole and competent and functional, when in fact his days were marked out by the habits of rising late, avoiding work in the library, and leaving early for the pub. Any move or change would expose the pretense.

Just you and me. Just for a year.

I can't.

Fang heard alarms. If she stayed and tried to protect Caitlin, her presence might drive James to some extreme. Or Fang might be drawn more deeply into their dysfunction. She didn't know if she could survive that. The thing Fang was best at was saving herself. So she went to America alone.

• • •

There was a second body covered with fungus. Number fifteen. Loren.

Either the fungus was contained, restricted to these two, or more likely it had already spread. But how? The bodysuits showed no faults, no breaches. They were isolated from each other, with no pathways for infection. The only possible connection would be through the air supply, and the scrubbers should remove any pathogens, certainly anything as large as a fungus.

In any case, it was bad. She could try rousing another steward manually. But to what purpose? Only she had the expertise to deal with this.

She realized she thought of it because she was desperately lonely. She wanted company with this problem. She wasn't going to get any.

Not enough fat to rouse. Increase glycogen uptake? Maybe, but carbohydrate fasting was a key part of the process.

They had this advantage over natural hibernators: they didn't need to get all their energy from stored body fat. Lipids were dripped in dermally to provide ATP. But body fat was getting metabolized anyway.

Signaling. Perhaps the antisenescents were signaling the fungus not to die. Slowing not its growth but its morbidity. If it were a fungus. Sure it was, it had to be. But confirm it.

• • •

After she came to the Lab, Fang learned that her adoption was not so much a matter of her initiative, or of Caitlin's, or of good fortune. Roger had pulled strings every step of the way—strings Fang had no idea existed.

He'd known of Fang because all student work—every paper, test, e-mail, click, eyeblink, keystroke—was stored and tracked and mined. Her permanent record. Corps and labs had algorithms conducting eternal worldwide surveillance for, among so many other things, promising scientists. Roger had his own algorithms: his stock-market eye for early bloomers, good draft choices. He'd purchased Fang's freedom from some Chinese consortium and linked her to Caitlin.

Roger, Fang came to realize, had seen in Caitlin's needs and infirmities a way to help three people: Caitlin, who needed someone to nurture and give herself to, so as not to immolate herself; Fang, who needed that nurturing; and himself, who needed Fang's talent. In other words: Roger judged that Caitlin would do best as the mother of a scientist.

He wasn't wrong. Caitlin's nurture was going to waste on James, who simply sucked it in and gave nothing back. And Fang needed a brilliant, loving, female example to give her confidence in her own brilliance, and learn the toughness she'd need to accomplish her work. That's what Caitlin herself had lacked.

If Fang had known all this, she'd have taken the terms; she'd have done anything to get out of China. But she hadn't known; she hadn't been consulted. So when she found out, she was furious. For Caitlin, for herself. As she saw it, Roger couldn't have the mother, so he took the daughter. He used their love and mutual need to get what he wanted, and then he broke them apart. It was cold and calculating and utterly selfish of Roger; of the three of them, only he wasn't damaged by it. She'd almost quit Gypsy in her fury.

She did quit the Lab. She went into product development at Glaxo, under contract to DARPA. That was the start of her hibernation work. It was for battlefield use, as a way to keep injured soldiers alive during transport. When she reflected on this move, she wasn't so sure that Roger hadn't pulled more strings. In any case, the work was essential to Gypsy.

Roger had fury of his own, to spare. Fang knew all about the calm front. Roger reeked of it. He'd learned that he had the talent and the position to do great harm; the orbiting bombs were proof of that. His anger and disappointment had raised in him the urge to do more harm. At the Lab he was surrounded by the means and the opportunity. So he'd gathered all his ingenuity and his rage against humanity and sequestered it in a project large enough and complex enough to occupy it fully, so that it could not further harm him or the world: Gypsy. He would do a thing that had never been done before; and he would take away half the bombs he'd enabled in the doing of it; and the thing would not be shared with humanity. She imagined he saw it as a victimless revenge.

Well, here were the victims.

• • •

A day later, *Pseudogymnoascus destructans* was her best guess. Or some mutation of it. It had killed most of the bats on Earth. It grew only in low temperatures, in the 4–15°C range. The ship was normally held at 4°C.

She could synthesize an antifungal agent with the gene printer, but what about interactions? Polyenes would bind with a fungus's ergosterols but could have severe and lethal side effects.

She thought about the cocktail. How she might tweak it. Sirtuins. Fibroplast growth factor 21. Hibernation induction trigger. [D-Ala^2, D-Leu^5]-Enkephalin. Pancreatic triacylglycerol lipase. 5'-adenosine monophosphate. Ghrelin. 3-iodothyronamine. Alpha2-macroglobulin. Carnosine, other antisenescents, antioxidants.

Some components acted only at the start of the process. They triggered a cascade of enzymes in key pathways to bring on torpor. Some continued to drip in, to reinforce gene expression, to suppress circadian rhythms, and so on.

It was all designed to interact with nonhuman mammalian genes she'd spliced in. Including parts of the bat immune system—*Myotis lucifugus*—parts relevant to hibernation, to respond to the appropriate mRNA signals. But were they also vulnerable to this fungus? *O God, did I do this? Did I open up this vulnerability?*

• • •

She gave her presentation, in the open, to DARPA. It was amazing; she was speaking in code to the few Gypsies in the audience, including Roger, telling them in effect how they'd survive the long trip to Alpha, yet her plaintext words were telling DARPA about battlefield applications: suspending wounded soldiers, possibly in space, possibly for long periods, 3D-printing organs, crisping stem cells, and so on.

In Q&A she knew DARPA was sold; they'd get their funding. Roger was right: everything was dual use.

• • •

She'd been up for ten days. The cramped, dark space was wearing her down. Save them. They had to make it. She'd pulled a DNA sequencer and a gene printer from the storage bay. As she fed it *E. coli* and *Mycoplasma mycoides* stock, she reviewed what she'd come up with.

She could mute the expression of the bat genes at this stage, probably without disrupting hibernation. They were the receptors for the triggers that started and stopped the process. But that could compromise rousing. So mute them temporarily—for how long?—hope to revive an immune response, temporarily damp down the antisenescents, add an antifungal. She'd have to automate everything in the mixture; the ship wouldn't rouse her a second time to supervise.

It was a long shot, but so was everything now.

It was too hard for her. For anyone. She had the technology: a complete library of genetic sequences, a range of restriction enzymes, Sleeping Beauty transposase, et cetera. She'd be capable on the spot, for instance, of producing a pathogen that could selectively kill individuals with certain ethnic markers—that had been one project at the Lab, demurely called "preventive." But she didn't have the knowledge she needed for this. It had taken years of research experimentation, and collaboration, to come up with the original cocktail, and it would take years more to truly solve this. She had only a few days. Then the residue of the cocktail would be out of her system and she would lose the ability to rehibernate. So she had to go with what she had now. Test it on DNA from her own saliva.

• • •

Not everyone stuck with Gypsy. One scientist at the Lab, Sidney Lefebvre, was wooed by Roger to sign up, and declined only after carefully studying their plans for a couple of weeks.

It's too hard, Roger. What you have here is impressive. But it's only a start. There are too many intractable problems. Much more work needs to be done.

That work won't get done. Things are falling apart, not coming together. It's now or never.

Regardless, the time for this is not now. This, too, will fall apart.

●●●

She wrote the log for the next steward, who would almost surely have the duty of more corpses. Worse, as stewards died, maintenance would be deferred. Systems would die. She didn't know how to address that. Maybe Lefebvre was right. But no: they had to make it. How could this be any harder than getting from Guangxhou to Dublin?

She prepared to go back under. Fasted the day. Enema, shower. Taps and stents and waldos and derms attached and the bodysuit sealed around her. She felt the cocktail run into her veins.

The lights were off. The air was chill. In her last moment of clarity, she stared into blackness. Always she had run, away from distress, toward something new, to eradicate its pain and its hold. Not from fear. As a gesture of contempt, of power: done with you, never going back. But run to where? No world, no O, no gravity, no hold, nothing to cling to. This was the end of the line. There was nowhere but here. And, still impossibly far, another forty-four years, Alpha C. As impossibly far as Earth.

3.

Roger recruited his core group face to face. At conferences and symposia he sat for papers that had something to offer his project, and he made a judgment about the presenter. If favorable, it led to a conversation. Always outside, in the open. Fire roads in the Berkeley hills. A cemetery in Zurich. The shores of Lake Como. Fry was well known, traveled much. He wasn't Einstein, he wasn't Feynman, he wasn't Hawking, but he had a certain presence.

The conferences were Kabuki. Not a scientist in the world was unlinked to classified projects through government or corporate sponsors. Presentations were so oblique that expert interpretation was required to parse their real import.

Roger parsed well. Within a year he had a few dozen trusted collaborators. They divided the mission into parts: target selection, engine and fuel, vessel, hibernation, navigation, obstacle avoidance, computers, deceleration, landfall, survival.

The puzzle had too many pieces. Each piece was unthinkably complex. They needed much more help.

They put up a site they called Gypsy. On the surface it was a gaming site, complex and thick with virtual worlds, sandboxes, self-evolving puzzles, and links. Buried in there was an interactive starship-design section, where ideas were solicited, models built, simulations run. Good nerdy crackpot fun.

The core group tested the site themselves for half a year before going live. Their own usage stats became the profile of the sort of visitors they sought: people like themselves: people with enough standing to have access to the high-speed classified web, with enough autonomy to waste professional time on a game site, and finally with enough curiosity and dissidence to pursue certain key links down a critical chain. They needed people far enough inside an institution to have access to resources, but not so far inside as to identify with its ideology. When a user appeared to fit that profile, a public key was issued. The key unlocked further levels and ultimately enabled secure e-mail to an encrypted server.

No one, not even Roger Fry, knew how big the conspiracy was. Ninety-nine percent of their traffic was noise—privileged kids, stoked hackers, drunken PhDs, curious spooks. Hundreds of keys were issued in the first year. Every key increased the risk. But without resources they were going nowhere.

The authorities would vanish Roger Fry and everyone associated with him on the day they learned what he was planning. Not because of the what: a starship posed no threat. But because of the how and the why: only serious and capable dissidents could plan so immense a thing; the seriousness and the capability were the threat. And eventually they would be found, because every bit of the world's digital traffic was swept up and stored and analyzed. There was a city under the Utah desert where these yottabytes of data were archived. But the sheer size of the archive outran its analysis and opened a time window in which they might act.

Some ran propellant calculations. Some forwarded classified medical studies. Some were space workers with access to shuttles and tugs. Some passed on classified findings from telescopes seeking exoplanets.

One was an operator of the particle beam at Shackleton Crater. The beam was used, among other purposes, to move the orbiting sleds containing the very bombs Roger had helped design.

One worked at a seed archive in Norway. She piggybacked a capsule into Earth orbit containing seeds from fifty thousand unmodified plant species, including plants legally extinct. They needed those because every cultivated acre on Earth was now planted with engineered varieties that were sterile; terminator genes had been implanted to protect the agro firms' profit streams; and these genes had jumped to wild varieties. There wasn't a live food plant left anywhere on Earth that could propagate itself.

They acquired frozen zygotes of some ten thousand animal species, from bacteria to primates. Hundred thousands more complete DNA sequences in a data library, and a genome printer. Nothing like the genetic diversity of Earth, even in its present state, but enough, perhaps, to reboot such diversity.

At Roger's lab, panels of hydrogenous carbon-composite, made to shield high-orbit craft from cosmic rays and to withstand temperatures of 2000 C, went missing. Quite a lot of silica aerogel as well.

At a sister lab, a researcher put them in touch with a contractor from whom they purchased, quite aboveboard, seventy kilometers of lightweight, high-current-density superconducting cable.

After a year, Roger decided that their web had grown too large to remain secure. He didn't like the number of unused keys going out. He didn't like the page patterns he was seeing. He didn't consult with the others, he just shut it down.

But they had their pieces.

SERGEI (2118)

Eat, drink, shit. That's all he did for the first day or three. Water tasted funny. Seventy-seven years might have viled it, or his taste buds. Life went on, including the ending of it. Vital signs of half the crew were flat. He considered disposing of bodies, ejecting them, but number one, he couldn't be sure they were dead; number two, he couldn't propel them hard enough to keep them from making orbit around the ship, which was funny but horrible; and finally, it would be unpleasant and very hard work that would tire him out. An old man—he surely felt old, and the calendar would back him up—needs to conserve his strength. So he let them lie on their slabs.

The logs told a grim story. They were slow. To try to make up for lost time, Sophie had reprogrammed the magsail to deploy later and to run at higher current. Another steward had been wakened at the original deployment point, to confirm their speed and position, and to validate the decision to wait. Sergei didn't agree with that, and he especially didn't like the handwaving over when to ignite the nuclear rocket in-system, but it was done: they'd gone the extra years at speed and now they needed to start decelerating hard.

CURRENT INJECTION FAILED. MAGSAIL NOT DEPLOYED.

He tapped the screen to cycle through its languages. Stopped at the Cyrillic script, and tapped the speaker, just so he could hear spoken Russian.

So he had to fix the magsail. Current had flowed on schedule from inside, but the sail wasn't charging or deploying. According to telltales, the bay was open but the superconducting cable just sat there. That meant EVA. He didn't like it, but there was no choice. It's what he was here for. Once it was done he'd shower again under that pathetic lukewarm stream, purge his bowels, get back in the mylar suit and go under for another, what, eight more years, a mere nothing, we're almost there. Ghost Planet Hope.

He was the only one onboard who'd been a career astronaut. Roger had conveyed a faint class disapproval about that, but needed the expertise. Sergei had been one of the gene-slushed orbital jockeys who pushed bomb sleds around. He knew the feel of zero g, of sunlight on one side of you and absolute cold on the other. He knew how it felt when the particle beam from Shackleton swept over you to push you and the sleds into a new orbit. And you saluted and cut the herds, and kept whatever more you might know to yourself.

Which in Sergei's case was quite a bit. Sergei knew orbital codes and protocols far beyond his pay grade; he could basically move anything in orbit to or from anywhere. But only Sergei, so Sergei thought, knew that. How Roger learned it remained a mystery.

To his great surprise, Sergei learned that even he hadn't known the full extent of his skills. How easy it had been to steal half a million bombs. True, the eternal war economy was so corrupt that materiel was supposed to disappear; something was wrong if it didn't. Still, he would never have dared anything so outrageous on his own. Despite Roger's planning, he was sweating the day he moved the first sled into an unauthorized orbit. But days passed, then weeks and months, as sled followed sled into new holding orbits. In eighteen months they had all their fuel. No traps had sprung, no alarms tripped. Sophie managed to make the manifests look okay. And he wondered again at what the world had become. And what he was in it.

This spacesuit was light, thin, too comfortable. Like a toddler's fleece playsuit with slippers and gloves. Even the helmet was soft. He was used to heavy Russian engineering, but whatever. They'd argued over whether to include a suit at all. He'd argued against. EVA had looked unlikely, an unlucky possibility. So he was happy now to have anything.

The soles and palms were sticky, a clever off-the-shelf idea inspired by lizards. Billions of carbon nanotubes lined them. The Van der Waals molecular force made them stick to any surface. He tested it by walking on the interior walls. Hands or feet held you fast, with or against the ship's rotational gravity. You had to kind of toe-and-heel to walk, but it was easy enough.

Пойдем. Let's go. He climbed into the hatch and cycled it. As the pressure dropped, the suit expanded and felt more substantial. He tested the grip of his palms on the hull before rising fully out of the hatch. Then his feet came up and gripped, and he stood.

In darkness and immensity stiller than he could comprehend. Interstellar space. The frozen splendor of the galactic core overhead. Nothing appeared to move.

He remembered a still evening on a lake, sitting with a friend on a dock, legs over the edge. They talked as the sky darkened, looking up as the stars came out. Only when it was fully dark did he happen to look down. The water was so still, stars were reflected under his feet. He almost lurched over the edge of the dock in surprise.

The memory tensed his legs, and he realized the galactic core was rotating slowly around the ship. Here on the outside of the ship its spin-induced gravity was reversed. He stood upright but felt pulled toward the stars.

He faced forward. One tenth of a light-year from Alpha, its two stars still appeared as one. They were brighter than Venus in the Earth's sky. They cast his faint but distinct shadow on the hull.

They were here. They had come this far. On this tiny splinter of human will forging through vast, uncaring space. It was remarkable.

A line of light to his left flashed. Some microscopic particle ionized by the ship's magnetic shield. He tensed again at this evidence of their movement and turned slowly, directing his beam over the hull. Its light caught a huge gash through one of the hydrogen tanks. Edges of the gash had failed to be covered by a dozen geckos, frozen in place by hydrogen ice. That was bad. Worse, it hadn't been in the log. Maybe it was from the impact Sophie had referred to. He would have to see how bad it was after freeing the magsail.

He turned, and toed and heeled his way carefully aft. Now ahead of him was our Sun, still one of the brightest stars, the heavens turning slowly around it. He approached the circular bay that held the magsail. His light showed six large spools of cable, each a meter and a half across and a meter thick. About five metric tons in all, seventy kilometers of thin superconductor wire. Current injection should have caused the spools to unreel under the force of the electric field. But it wasn't getting current, or it was somehow stuck. He was going to have to . . . well, he wasn't sure.

Then he saw it. Almost laughed at the simplicity and familiarity of it. Something like a circuit breaker, red and green buttons, the red one lit. He squatted at the edge of the bay and found he could reach the thing. He felt cold penetrate his suit. He really ought to go back inside and spend a few hours troubleshooting, read the fucking manual, but the cold and the flimsy spacesuit and the immensity convinced him otherwise. He slapped the green button.

It lit. The cable accepted current. He saw it lurch. As he smiled and stood, the current surging in the coils sent its field through the soles of his spacesuit, disrupting for a moment the molecular force holding them to the hull. In that moment, the angular velocity of the rotating ship was transmitted to his body and he detached, moving away from the ship at a stately three meters per second. Beyond his flailing feet, the cables of the magsail began leisurely to unfurl.

As he tumbled the stars rolled past. He'd seen Orion behind the ship in the moment he detached, and as he tumbled he looked for it, for something to grab on to, but he never saw it or the ship again. So he didn't see the huge coil of wire reach its full extension, nor the glow of ionization around the twenty-kilometer circle when it began to drag against the interstellar medium, nor how the ship itself started to lag against the background stars. The ionization set up a howl across the radio spectrum, but his radio was off, so he didn't hear that. He tumbled in silence in the bowl of the heavens at his fixed velocity, which was now slightly greater than the ship's. Every so often the brightness of Alpha crossed his view. He was going to get there first.

4.

Their biggest single problem was fuel. To cross that enormous distance in less than a human lifetime, even in this stripped-down vessel, required an inconceivable amount of energy. Ten to the twenty-first joules. 250 trillion kilowatt hours. Twenty years' worth of all Earth's greedy energy consumption. The mass of the fuel, efficient though it was, would be several times the mass of the ship. And to reach cruising speed was only half of it; they had to decelerate when they reached Alpha C, which doubled the fuel budget. It was undoable.

Until someone found an old paper on magnetic sails. A superconducting loop of wire many kilometers across, well charged, could act as a drag brake against the interstellar medium. That would cut the fuel requirement almost in half. Done that way, it was just possible, though out on the ragged edge of what was survivable. This deceleration would take ten years.

For their primary fuel, Roger pointed to the hundreds of thousands of bombs in orbit. His bombs. His intellectual property. Toss them out the back and ignite them. A Blumlein pulse-forming line—they called it the "bloom line"—a self-generated magnetic vise, something like a Z-pinch—would direct nearly all the blast to exhaust velocity. The vise, called into being for the nanoseconds of ignition, funneled all that force straight back. Repeat every minute. Push the compression ratio up, you won't get many neutrons; neutrons were bad for living things.

In the end they had two main engines: first, the antiproton-fusion monster to get them up to speed. It could only be used for the first year; any longer and the antiprotons would decay. The magsail would slow them down as they approached the system.

For the last leg they had a gas-core nuclear rocket, to decelerate in the system. It required carrying a large amount of hydrogen. They discussed scooping hydrogen from the interstellar medium as they traveled, but Roger vetoed it: not off the shelf. They didn't have the time or means to devise a new technology. Anyway, the hydrogen would make, in combination with their electromagnetic shield, an effective barrier to cosmic rays. Dual use.

And even so, everything had to be stretched to the limit: the mass of the ship minimized, the human lifetime lengthened, the fuel leveraged every way possible.

The first spacecraft ever to leave the solar system, Pioneer 10, had used Jupiter's gravity to boost its velocity. As it flew by, it stole kinetic energy from the giant planet; its small mass sped up a lot; Jupiter's stupendous mass slowed unnoticeably.

They would do the same thing to lose speed. They had the combined mass of two stars orbiting each other, equal to two thousand Jupiters. When *Gypsy* was to arrive in 2113, the stars in their mutual orbit would be as close together as they ever got: 11 astronomical units. *Gypsy* would fly by the B star and pull one last trick: retrofire the nuclear rocket deep in its gravity well; that would multiply the kinetic effect of the propellant severalfold. And then they'd repeat that maneuver around A. The relative closeness of 11 AU was still as far as Earth to Saturn, so even after arrival, even at their still-great speed, the dual braking maneuver would take over a year.

Only then would they be moving slowly enough to aerobrake in the planet's atmosphere, and that would take a few dozen passes before they could ride the ship down on its heatshield to the surface.

If there was a planet. If it had an atmosphere.

ZIA (2120)

As a child he was lord of the dark—finding his way at night, never stumbling, able to read books by starlight; to read also, in faces and landscapes, traces and glimmers that others missed. Darkness was warmth and comfort to him.

A cave in Ephesus. In the Q'uran, Surah Al-Kahf. The sleepers waking after centuries, emerging into a changed world. Trying to spend old coins.

After the horror of his teen years, he'd found that dark was still a friend. Looking through the eyepiece of an observatory telescope, in the Himalayan foothills, in Uttar Pradesh. Describing the cluster of galaxies, one by one, to the astronomer. *You see the seventh? What eyes!*

Nothing moved but in his mind. Dreams of tenacity and complication. Baffling remnants, consciousness too weak to sort. Every unanswered question of his life, every casual observation, every bit of mental flotsam, tossed together in one desperate, implicate attempt at resolving them all. Things fell; he lunged to catch them. He stood on street corners in an endless night, searching for his shoes, his car, his keys, his wife. His mother chided him in a room lit by incandescent bulbs, dim and flickering like firelight. Galaxies in the eyepiece faded, and he looked up from the eyepiece to a blackened sky. He lay waking, in the dark, now aware of the dream state, returning with such huge reluctance to the life of the body, that weight immovable on its slab.

His eyelid was yanked open. A drop of fluid splashed there. A green line swept across his vision. He caught a breath and it burned in his lungs.

He was awake. Aboard *Gypsy*. It was bringing him back to life.

But I'm cold. Too cold to shiver. Getting colder as I wake up.

How hollow he felt. In this slight gravity. How unreal. It came to him, in the eclipsing of his dreams and the rising of his surroundings, that the gravity of Earth might be something more profound than the acceleration of a mass, the curvature of spacetime. Was it not an emanation of the planet, a life force? All life on Earth evolved in it, rose from it, fought it every moment, lived and bred and died awash in it. Those tides swept through our cells, the force from Earth, and the gravity of the sun and the gravity of the moon. What was life out here, without that embrace, that permeation, that bondage? Without it, would they wither and die like plants in a shed?

The hollowness came singing, roaring, whining, crackling into his ears. Into his throat and nose and eyes and skin it came as desiccation. Searing into his mouth. He needed to cough and he couldn't. His thorax spasmed.

There was an antiseptic moistness in his throat. It stung, but his muscles has loosened. He could breathe. Cold swept from his shoulders down through his torso and he began to shiver uncontrollably.

When he could, he raised a hand. He closed his eyes and held the hand afloat in the parodic gravity, thinking about it, how it felt, how far away it actually was. At last, with hesitation, his eyes opened and came to focus. An old man's hand, knobby, misshapen at the joints, the skin papery, sagging and hanging in folds. He couldn't close the fingers. How many years had he slept? He forced on his hand the imagination of a clenched fist. The hand didn't move.

Oh my god the pain.

Without which, no life. Pain too is an emanation of the planet, of the life force.

It sucked back like a wave, gathering for another concussion. He tried to sit up and passed out.

• • •

Nikos Kakopoulos was a short man, just over five feet, stocky but fit. The features of his face were fleshy, slightly comic. He was graying, balding, but not old. In his fifties. He smiled as he said he planned to be around a hundred years from now. His office was full of Mediterranean light. A large Modigliani covered one wall. His money came mostly from aquifer rights. He spent 10 percent of it on charities. One such awarded science scholarships. Which is how he'd come to Roger's attention.

So you see, I am not such a bad guy,

Those foundations are just window dressing. What they once called greenwash.

Zia, said Roger.

Kakopoulos shrugged as if to say, Let him talk, I've heard it all. To Zia he said: They do some good after all. They're a comfort to millions of people.

Drinking water would be more of a comfort.

There isn't enough to go round. I didn't create that situation.

You exploit it.

So sorry to say this. Social justice and a civilized lifestyle can't be done both at once. Not for ten billion people. Not on this planet.

You've decided this.

It's a conclusion based on the evidence.

And you care about this why?

I'm Greek. We invented justice and civilization.

You're Cypriot. Also, the Chinese would argue that. The Persians. The Egyptians. Not to mention India.

Kakopoulos waved away the first objection and addressed the rest. Of course they would. And England, and Germany, and Italy, and Russia, and the US. They're arguing as we speak. Me, I'm not going to argue. I'm going to a safe place until the arguing is over. After that, if we're very lucky, we can have our discussion about civilization and justice.

On your terms.

On terms that might have some meaning.

What terms would those be?

World population under a billion, for starters. Kakopoulos reached across the table and popped an olive into his mouth.

How do you think that's going to happen? asked Zia.

It's happening. Just a matter of time. Since I don't know how much time, I want a safe house for the duration.

How are you going to get up there?

Kakopoulos grinned. *When the Chinese acquired Lockheed, I picked up an X-33. It can do Mach 25. I have a spaceport on Naxos. Want a ride?*

The VTOL craft looked like the tip of a Delta IV rocket, or of a penis: a blunt, rounded conic. Not unlike Kakopoulos himself. Some outsize Humpty Dumpty.

How do you know him? Zia asked Roger as they boarded.

I've been advising him.

You're advising the man who owns a third of the world's fresh water?

He owns a lot of things. My first concern is for our project. We need him.

What for?

Roger stared off into space.

He immiserates the Earth, Roger.

We all ten billion immiserate the Earth by being here.

Kakopoulos returned.

Make yourselves comfortable. Even at Mach 25, it takes some time.

It was night, and the Earth was below their window. Rivers of manmade light ran across it. Zia could see the orange squiggle of the India-Pakistan border, all three thousand floodlit kilometers of it. Then the ship banked and the window turned to the stars.

Being lord of the dark had a touch of clairvoyance in it. The dark seldom brought surprise to him. Something bulked out there and he felt it. Some gravity about it called to him from some future. Sun blazed forth behind the limb of the Earth, but the thing was still in Earth's shadow. It made a blackness against the Milky Way. Then sunlight touched it. Its lines caught light: the edges of panels, tanks, heat sinks, antennas. Blunt radar-shedding angles. A squat torus shape under it all. It didn't look like a ship. It looked like a squashed donut to which a junkyard had been glued. It turned slowly on its axis.

My safe house, said Kakopoulos.

It was, indeed, no larger than a house. About ten meters long, twice that across. It had cost a large part of Kakopoulos's considerable fortune. Which he recouped by manipulating and looting several central banks. As a result, a handful of small countries, some hundred million people, went off the cliff-edge of modernity into an abyss of debt peonage.

While they waited to dock with the thing, Kakopoulos came and sat next to Zia.

Listen, my friend—

I'm not your friend.

As you like, I don't care. I don't think you're stupid. When I said my foundations make people feel better, I meant the rich, of course. You're Pakistani?

Indian actually.

But Muslim. Kashmir?

Zia shrugged.

Okay. We're not so different, I think. I grew up in the slums of Athens after the euro collapsed. The histories, the videos, they don't capture it. I imagine Kashmir was much worse. But we each found a way out, no? So tell me, would you go back to that? No, you don't have to answer. You wouldn't. Not for anything. You'd sooner die. But you're not the kind of asshole who writes conscience checks. Or thinks your own self is wonderful enough to deserve anything. So where does that leave a guy like you in this world?

Fuck you.

Kakopoulos patted Zia's hand and smiled. I love it when people say fuck you to me. You know why? It means I won. They've got nothing left but their fuck you. He got up and went away.

The pilot came in then, swamp-walking the zero g in his velcro shoes, and said they'd docked.

The ship massed about a hundred metric tons. A corridor circled the inner circumference, floor against the outer hull, most of the space taken up by hibernation slabs for a crew of twenty. Once commissioned, it would spin on its axis a few times a minute to create something like lunar gravity. They drifted through it slowly, pulling themselves by handholds.

This, Kakopoulos banged a wall, is expensive. Exotic composites, all that aerogel. Why so much insulation?

Roger let "expensive" pass unchallenged. Zia didn't.

You think there's nothing more important than money.

Kakopoulos turned, as if surprised Zia was still there. He said, There are many things more important than money. You just don't get any of them without it.

Roger said, Even while you're hibernating, the ship will radiate infrared. That's one reason you'll park at a Lagrange point, far enough away not to attract attention. When you wake up and start using energy, you're going to light up like a Christmas tree. And you're going to hope that whatever is left on Earth or in space won't immediately blow you out of the sky. This insulation will hide you somewhat.

At one end of the cramped command center was a micro-apartment.

What's this, Nikos?

Ah, my few luxuries. Music, movies, artworks. We may be out here awhile after we wake up. Look at my kitchen.

A range?

Propane, but it generates 30,000 BTU!

That's insane. You're not on holiday here.

Look, it's vented, only one burner, I got a great engineer, you can examine the plans—

Get rid of it.

What! Kakopoulos yelled. Whose ship is this!

Roger pretended to think for a second. Do you mean who owns it, or who designed it?

Do you know how much it cost to get that range up here?

I can guess to the nearest million.

When I wake up I want a good breakfast!

When you wake up you'll be too weak to stand. Your first meal will be coming down tubes.

Kakopoulos appeared to sulk.

Nikos, what is your design specification here?

I just want a decent omelette.

I can make that happen. But the range goes.

Kakopoulos nursed his sulk, then brightened. Gonna be some meteor, that range. I'll call my observatory, have them image it.

Later, when they were alone, Zia said: All right, Roger. I've been very patient.

Patient? Roger snorted.

How can that little pustule help us?
That's our ship. We're going to steal it.
Later, Zia suggested that they christen the ship the Fuck You.

•••

Eighty years later, Zia was eating one of Kakopoulos's omelettes. Freeze-dried egg, mushrooms, onion, tarragon. Microwaved with two ounces of water. Not bad. He had another.

Mach 900, asshole, he said aloud.

Most of the crew were dead. Fungus had grown on the skin stretched like drums over their skulls, their ribs, their hips.

He'd seen worse. During his mandatory service, as a teenager in the military, he'd patrolled Deccan slums. He'd seen parents eating their dead children. Pariah dogs fat as sheep roamed the streets. Cadavers, bones, skulls, were piled in front of nearly every house. The cloying carrion smell never lifted. Hollowed-out buildings housed squatters and corpses equally, darkened plains of them below fortified bunkers lit like Las Vegas, where the driving bass of party music echoed the percussion of automatic weapons and rocket grenades.

Now his stomach rebelled, but he commanded it to be still as he swallowed some olive oil. Gradually the chill in his core subsided.

He needed to look at the sky. The ship had two telescopes: a one-meter honeycomb mirror for detail work and a wide-angle high-res CCD camera. Zoomed fully out, the camera took in about eighty degrees. Ahead was the blazing pair of Alpha Centauri A and B, to the eye more than stars but not yet suns. He'd never seen anything like them. Brighter than Venus, bright as the full moon, but such tiny disks. As he watched, the angle of them moved against the ship's rotation.

He swept the sky, looking for landmarks. But the stars were wrong. What had happened to Orion? Mintaka had moved. The belt didn't point to Sirius, as it should. A brilliant blue star off Orion's left shoulder outshone Betelgeuse, and then he realized. *That* was Sirius. Thirty degrees from where it should be. Of course: it was only eight light-years from Earth. They had come half that distance, and, like a nearby buoy seen against a far shore, it had changed position against the farther stars.

More distant stars had also shifted, but not as much. He turned to what he still absurdly thought of as "north." The Big Dipper was there. The Little Dipper's bowl was squashed. Past Polaris was Cassiopeia, the zigzag W, the queen's throne. And there a new, bright star blazed above it, as if that W had grown another zag. Could it be a nova? He stared, and the stars of Cassiopeia circled this strange bright one slowly as the ship rotated. Then he knew: the strange star was Sol. Our Sun.

That was when he felt it, in his body: they were really here.

• • •

From the beginning Roger had a hand—a heavy, guiding hand—in the design of the ship. Not for nothing had he learned the Lab's doctrine of dual use. Not for nothing had he cultivated Kakopoulos's acquaintance. Every feature that fitted the ship for interstellar space was a plausible choice for Kak's purpose: hibernators, cosmic-ray shielding, nuclear rocket, hardened computers, plutonium pile and Stirling engine.

In the weeks prior to departure, they moved the ship to a more distant orbit, too distant for Kak's X-33 to reach. There they jettisoned quite a bit of the ship's interior. They added their fusion engine, surrounded the vessel with fuel sleds, secured antiproton traps, stowed the magsail, loaded the seed bank and a hundred other things.

• • •

They were three hundred AU out from Alpha Centauri. Velocity was one thousandth c. The magsail was programmed to run for two more years, slowing them by half again. But lately their deceleration had shown variance. The magsail was running at higher current than planned. Very close to max spec. That wasn't good. Logs told him why, and that was worse.

He considered options, none good. The sail was braking against the interstellar medium, stray neutral atoms of hydrogen. No one knew for sure how it would behave once it ran into Alpha's charged solar wind. Nor just where that wind started. The interstellar medium might already be giving way to it. If so, the count of galactic cosmic rays would be going down and the temperature of charged particles going up.

He checked. Definitely maybe on both counts.

He'd never liked this plan, its narrow margins of error. Not that he had a better. That was the whole problem: no plan B. Every intricate, fragile, untried part of it had to work. He'd pushed pretty hard for a decent margin of error in this deceleration stage and the subsequent maneuvering in the system—what a tragedy it would be to come to grief so close, within sight of shore—and now he saw that margin evaporating.

Possibly the sail would continue to brake in the solar wind. If only they could have tested it first.

Zia didn't trust materials. Or, rather: he trusted them to fail. Superconductors, carbon composite, silicon, the human body. Problem was, you never knew just how or when they'd fail.

One theory said that a hydrogen wall existed somewhere between the termination shock and the heliopause, where solar wind gave way to interstellar space. Three hundred AU put *Gypsy* in that dicey zone.

It would be prudent to back off the magsail current. That would lessen their decel, and they needed all they could get, they had started it too late, but they also needed to protect the sail and run it as long as possible.

Any change to the current had to happen slowly. It would take hours, possibly days. The trick was not to deform the coil too much in the process, or create eddy currents that could quench the superconducting field.

The amount of power he had available was another issue. The plutonium running the Stirling engine had decayed to about half its original capacity.

He shut down heat in the cabin to divert more to the Stirling engine. He turned down most of the LED lighting, and worked in the semidark, except for the glow of the monitor. Programmed a gentle ramp up in current.

Then he couldn't keep his eyes open.

• • •

At Davos, he found himself talking to an old college roommate. Carter Hall III was his name; he was something with the UN now, and with the Council for Foreign Relations—an enlightened and condescending asshole. They were both Harvard '32, but Hall remained a self-appointed Brahmin, generously, sincerely, and with vast but guarded amusement, guiding a Sudra through the world that was his by birthright. Never mind the Sudra was Muslim.

From a carpeted terrace they overlooked a groomed green park. There was no snow in Davos this January, an increasingly common state of affairs. Zia noted but politely declined to point out the obvious irony, the connection between the policies determined here and the retreat of the snow line.

Why Zia was there was complicated. He was persona non grata with the ruling party, but he was a scientist, he had security clearances, and he had access to diplomats on both sides of the border. India had secretly built many thousands of microfusion weapons and denied it. The US was about to enter into the newest round of endless talks over "nonproliferation," in which the US never gave up anything but insisted that other nations must.

Hall now lectured him. India needed to rein in its population, which was over two billion. The US had half a billion.

Zia, please, look at the numbers. Four children per household just isn't sustainable.

Abruptly Zia felt his manners fail.

Sustainable? Excuse me. Our Indian culture is four thousand years old, self-sustained through all that time. Yours is two, three, maybe five hundred years old, depending on your measure. And in that short time, not only is it falling apart, it's taking the rest of the world down with it, including my homeland.

Two hundred years, I don't get that, if you mean Western—
I mean technology, I mean capital, I mean extraction.

Well, but those are very, I mean if you look at your, your four thousand years of, of poverty and class discrimination, and violence—

Ah? And there is no poverty or violence in your brief and perfect history? No extermination? No slavery?

Hall's expression didn't change much.

We've gotten past all that, Zia. We—

Zia didn't care that Hall was offended. He went on:

The story of resource extraction has only two cases, okay? In the first case, the extractors arrive and make the local ruler an offer. Being selfish, he takes it and he becomes rich—never so rich as the extractors, but compared to his people, fabulously, delusionally rich. His people become the cheap labor used to extract the resource. This leads to social upheaval. Villages are moved, families destroyed. A few people are enriched, the majority are ruined. Maybe there is an uprising against the ruler.

In the second case the ruler is smarter. Maybe he's seen some neighboring ruler's head on a pike. He says no thanks to the extractors. To this they have various responses: make him a better offer, find a greedier rival, hire an assassin, or bring in the gunships. But in the end it's the same: a few people are enriched, most are ruined. What the extractors never, ever do in any case, in all your history, is take no for an answer.

Zia, much as I enjoy our historical discussions—

Ah, you see? There it is—your refusal to take no. Talk is done, now we move forward with your agenda.

We have to deal with the facts on the ground. Where we are now.

Yes, of course. It's remarkable how, when the mess you've made has grown so large that even you must admit to it, you want to reset everything to zero. You want to get past "all that." All of history starts over, with these "facts on the ground." Let's move on, move forward, forget how we got here, forget the exploitation and the theft and the waste and the betrayals. Forget the, what is that charming accounting word, the externalities. Start from the new zero.

Hall looked weary and annoyed that he was called upon to suffer such childishness. That well-fed yet kept-fit form hunched, that pale skin looked suddenly papery and aged in the Davos sunlight.

You know, Zia prodded, *greed could at least be more efficient. If you know what you want, at least take it cleanly. No need to leave whole countries in ruins.*

Hall smiled a tight, grim smile, just a glimpse of the wolf beneath. He said: *Then it wouldn't be greed. Greed never knows what it wants.*

That was the exact measure of Hall's friendship, to say that to Zia. But then Zia knew what he wanted: out.

$$\bullet \bullet \bullet$$

As he drifted awake, he realized that, decades past, the ship would have collected data on the Sun's own heliopause on their way out. If he could access that data, maybe he could learn whether the hydrogen wall was a real thing. What effect it might—

There was a loud bang. The monitor and the cabin went dark. His mind reached into the outer darkness and it sensed something long and loose and broken trailing behind them.

What light there was came back on. The computer rebooted. The monitor displayed readings for the magsail over the past hour: current ramping up, then oscillating to compensate for varying densities in the medium, then a sharp spike. And then zero. Quenched.

Hydrogen wall? He didn't know. The magsail was fried. He tried for an hour more to get it to accept current. No luck. He remembered with some distaste the EVA suit. He didn't want to go outside, to tempt that darkness, but he might have to, so he walked forward to check it out.

The suit wasn't in its cubby. Zia turned and walked up the corridor, glancing at his torpid crewmates. The last slab was empty.

Sergei was gone. The suit was gone. You would assume they'd gone together, but that wasn't in the logs. *I may be some time.* Sergei didn't strike him as the type to take a last walk in the dark. And for that he wouldn't have needed the suit. Still. You can't guess what anyone might do.

So that was final: no EVA: the magsail couldn't be fixed. From the console, he cut it loose.

They were going far too fast. Twice what they'd planned. Now they had only the nuclear plasma rocket for deceleration, and one fuel tank was empty, somehow. Even though the fuel remaining outmassed the ship, it wasn't enough. If they couldn't slow below the escape velocity of the system, they'd shoot right through and out the other side.

The ship had been gathering data for months and had good orbital elements for the entire system. Around the A star were four planets, none in a position to assist with flybys. Even if they were, their masses would be little help. Only the two stars were usable.

If he brought them in a lot closer around B—how close could they get? one fiftieth AU? one hundredth?—and if the heat shield held—it should withstand 2500°C for a few hours—the ship could be slowed more with the same amount of fuel. The B star was closest: it was the less luminous of the pair, cooler, allowing them to get in closer, shed more speed. Then repeat the maneuver at A.

There was a further problem. Twelve years ago, as per the original plan, Alpha A and B were at their closest to one another: 11 AU. The stars were now twenty AU apart and widening. So the trip from B to A would take twice as long. And systems were failing. They were out on the rising edge of the bathtub curve.

Power continued erratic. The computer crashed again and again as he worked out the trajectories. He took to writing down intermediate results on paper in case he lost a session, cursing as he did so. Materials. We stole our tech from the most corrupt forces on Earth. Dude, you want an extended warranty with that? He examined the Stirling engine, saw that the power surge had compromised it. He switched the pile over to backup thermocouples. That took hours to do and it was less efficient, but it kept the computer running. It was still frustrating. The computer was designed to be redundant, hardened, hence slow. Minimal graphics, no 3D holobox. He had to think through his starting parameters carefully before he wasted processor time running a simulation.

Finally he had a new trajectory, swinging in perilously close to B, then A. It might work. Next he calculated that, when he did what he was about to do, seventy kilometers of magsail cable wouldn't catch them up and foul them. Then he fired the maneuvering thrusters.

• • •

What sold him, finally, was a handful of photons.

This is highly classified, said Roger. He held a manila file folder containing paper. Any computer file was permeable, hackable. Paper was serious.

The data were gathered by an orbiting telescope. It wasn't a photograph. It was a blurred, noisy image that looked like rings intersecting in a pond a few seconds after some pebbles had been thrown.

It's a deconvolved cross-correlation map of a signal gathered by a chopped pair of Bracewell baselines. You know how that works?

He didn't. Roger explained. From earth, any habitable planet around Alpha Centauri A or B would appear a small fraction of an arc-second away from the stars, and would be at least twenty-two magnitudes fainter. At that separation, the most sensitive camera made, with the best dynamic range, couldn't hope to find the planet in the stars' glare. But put several cameras together in a particular phase relation and the stars' light could be nulled out. What remained, if anything, would be light from another source. A planet, perhaps.

Also this, in visible light.

An elliptical iris of grainy red, black at its center, where an occulter had physically blocked the stars' disks.

Coronagraph, said Roger. Here's the detail.

A speck, a single pixel, slightly brighter than the enveloping noise.

What do you think?

Could be anything. Dust, hot pixel, cosmic ray . . .

It shows up repeatedly. And it moves.

Roger, for all I know you photoshopped it in.

He looked honestly shocked. Do you really think I'd . . .

I'm kidding. But where did you get these? Can you trust the source?

Why would anyone fake such a thing?

The question hung and around it gathered, like sepsis, the suspicion of some agency setting them up, of some agenda beyond their knowing. After the Kepler exoplanet finder went dark, subsequent exoplanet data—like all other government-sponsored scientific work—were classified. Roger's clearance was pretty high, but even he couldn't be sure of his sources.

You're not convinced, are you.

But somehow Zia was. The orbiting telescope had an aperture of, he forgot the final number, it had been scaled down several times owing to budget cuts. A couple of meters, maybe. That meant light from this far-off dim planet fell on it at a rate of just a few photons per second. It made him unutterably lonely to think of those photons traveling so far. It also made him believe in the planet.

Well, okay, Roger Fry was mad. Zia knew that. But he would throw in with Roger because all humanity was mad. Perhaps always had been. Certainly for the past century-plus, with the monoculture madness called modernity. Roger at least was mad in a different way, perhaps Zia's way.

●●●

He wrote the details into the log, reduced the orbital mechanics to a cookbook formula. Another steward would have to be awakened when they reached the B star; that would be in five years; his calculations weren't good enough to automate the burn time, which would depend on the ship's precise momentum and distance from the star as it rounded. It wasn't enough just to slow down; their exit trajectory from B needed to point them exactly to where A would be a year later. That wouldn't be easy; he took a couple of days to write an app to make it easier, but with large blocks of memory failing in the computer, Sophie's idea of a handwritten logbook no longer looked so dumb.

As he copied it all out, he imagined the world they'd left so far behind: the billions in their innocence or willed ignorance or complicity, the elites he'd despised for their lack of imagination, their surfeit of hubris, working together in a horrible *folie à deux.* He saw the bombs raining down, atomizing history and memory and accomplishment, working methodically backwards from the cities to the cradles of civilization to the birthplace of the species—the Fertile Crescent, the Horn of Africa, the Great Rift Valley—in a crescendo of destruction and denial of everything humanity had ever been—its failures, its cruelties, its grandeurs, its aspirations—all extirpated to the root, in a fury of self-loathing that fed on what it destroyed.

Zia's anger rose again in his ruined, aching body—his lifelong pointless rage at all that stupidity, cupidity, yes, there's some hollow satisfaction being away from all that. Away from the noise of their being. Their unceasing commotion of disruption and corruption. How he'd longed to escape it. But in the silent enclosure of the ship, in this empty house populated by the stilled ghosts of his crewmates, he now longed for any sound, any noise. He had wanted to be here, out in the dark. But not for nothing. And he wept.

And then he was just weary. His job was done. Existence seemed a pointless series of problems. What was identity? Better never to have been. He shut his eyes.

● ● ●

In bed with Maria, she moved in her sleep, rolled against him, and he rolled away. She twitched and woke from some dream.

What! What! she cried.

He flinched. His heart moved, but he lay still, letting her calm. Finally he said, What was that?

You pulled away from me!

Then they were in a park somewhere. Boston? Maria was yelling at him, in tears. Why must you be so negative!

● ● ●

He had no answer for her, then or now. Or for himself. Whatever "himself" might be. Something had eluded him in his life, and he wasn't going to find it now.

He thought again of Sergei. Well, it was still an option for him. He wouldn't need a suit.

Funny, isn't it, how one's human sympathy—Zia meant most severely his own—extends about as far as those most like oneself. He meant true sympathy; abstractions like justice don't count. Even now, missing Earth, he felt sympathy only for those aboard *Gypsy*, those orphaned, damaged, disaffected, dispossessed, Aspergerish souls whose anger at that great abstraction, The World, was more truly an anger at all those fortunate enough to be unlike them. We were all so young. How can you be so young, and so hungry for, yet so empty of life?

As he closed his log, he hit on a final option for the ship, if not himself. If after rounding B and A the ship still runs too fast to aerobrake into orbit around the planet, do this. Load all the genetic material—the frozen zygotes, the seed bank, the whatever—into a heatshielded pod. Drop it into the planet's atmosphere. If not themselves, some kind of life would have some chance. Yet as soon as he wrote those words, he felt their sting.

Roger, and to some degree all of them, had seen this as a way to transcend their thwarted lives on Earth. They were the essence of striving humanity: their planning and foresight served the animal's desperate drive to overcome what can't be overcome. To escape the limits of death. Yet transcendence, if it meant anything at all, was the accommodation to limits: a finding of freedom within them, not a breaking of them. Depositing the proteins of life here, like a stiff prick dropping its load, could only, in the best case, lead to a replication of the same futile striving. The animal remains trapped in the cage of its being.

5.

An old, old man in a wheelchair. Tube in his nose. Oxygen bottle on a cart. He'd been somebody at the Lab once. Recruited Roger, among many others, plucked him out of the pack at

Caltech. Roger loathed the old man but figured he owed him. And was owed.

They sat on a long, covered porch looking out at hills of dry grass patched with dark stands of live oak. The old man was feeling pretty spry after he'd thumbed through Roger's papers and lit the cigar Roger offered him. He detached the tube, took a discreet puff, exhaled very slowly, and put the tube back in.

Hand it to you, Roger, most elaborate, expensive form of mass suicide in history.

Really? I'd give that honor to the so-called statecraft of the past century.

Wouldn't disagree. But that's been very good to you and me. That stupidity gradient.

This effort is modest by comparison. Very few lives are at stake here. They might even survive it.

How many bombs you got onboard this thing? How many megatons?

They're not bombs, they're fuel. We measure it in exajoules.

Gonna blow them up in a magnetic pinch, aren't you? I call things that blow up bombs. But fine, measure it in horse-power if it makes you feel virtuous. Exajoules, huh? He stared into space for a minute. Ship's mass?

One hundred metric tons dry.

That's nice and light. Wonder where you got ahold of that. But you still don't have enough push. Take you over a hundred years. Your systems'll die.

Seventy-two years.

You done survival analysis? You get a bathtub curve with most of these systems. Funny thing is, redundancy works against you.

How so?

Shit, you got Sidney Lefebvre down the hall from you, world's expert in failure modes, don't you know that?

Roger knew the name. The man worked on something completely different now. Somehow this expertise had been erased from his resume and his working life.

How you gone slow down?

Magsail.

I always wondered, would that work.

You wrote the papers on it.

You know how hand-wavy they are. We don't know squat about the interstellar medium. And we don't have superconductors that good anyway. Or do we?

Roger didn't answer.

What happens when you get into the system?

That's what I want to know. Will the magsail work in the solar wind? Tarasenko says no.

Fuck him.

His math is sound. I want to know what you know. Does it work?

How would I know. Never got to test it. Never heard of anyone who did.

Tell me, Dan.

Tell you I don't know. Tarasenko's a crank, got a Ukraine-sized chip on his shoulder.

That doesn't mean he's wrong.

The old man shrugged, looked critically at the cigar, tapped the ash off its end.

Don't hold out on me.

Christ on a crutch, Roger, I'm a dead man. Want me to spill my guts, be nice, bring me a Havana.

There was a spell of silence. In the sunstruck sky a turkey vulture wobbled and banked into an updraft.

How you gone build a magsail that big? You got some superconductor scam goin'?

After ten years of braking we come in on this star, through its heliopause, at about five hundred kilometers per second. That's too fast to be captured by the system's gravity.

Cause I can help you there. Got some yttrium futures.

If we don't manage enough decel after that, we're done.

Gas-core reactor rocket.

We can't carry enough fuel. Do the math. Specific impulse is about three thousand at best.

The old man took the tube from his nose, tapped more ash off the cigar, inhaled. After a moment he began to cough. Roger had seen this act before. But it went on longer than usual, into a loud climax.

Roger . . . you really doin' this? Wouldn't fool a dead man?

I'm modeling. For a multiplayer game.

That brought the old man more than half back. Fuck you too, he said. But that was for any surveillance, Roger thought.

The old man stared into the distance, then said: Oberth effect.

What's that?

Here's what you do, the old man whispered, hunched over, as he brought out a pen and an envelope.

ROSA (2125)

After she'd suffered through the cold, the numbness, the chills, the burning, still she lay, unready to move, as if she weren't whole, had lost some essence—her anima, her purpose. She went over the whole mission in her mind, step by step, piece by piece. Do we have everything? The bombs to get us out of the solar system, the sail to slow us down, the nuclear rocket, the habitat . . . what else? What have we forgotten? There is something in the dark.

What is in the dark? Another ship? Oh my God. If we did it, they could do it, too. It would be insane for them to come after us. But they are insane. And we stole their bombs. What would they *not* do to us? Insane and vengeful as they are. They could send a drone after us, unmanned, or manned by a suicide crew. It's just what they would do.

She breathed the stale, cold air and stared up at the dark ceiling. Okay, relax. That's the worst-case scenario. Best case, they never saw us go. Most likely, they saw but they have other priorities. Everything has worked so far. Or you would not be lying here fretting, Rosa.

• • •

Born Rose. Mamá was from Trinidad. Dad was Venezuelan. She called him Papá against his wishes. Solid citizens, assimilated: a banker, a realtor. Home was Altadena, California. There was a bit of Irish blood and more than a dollop of Romany, the renegade uncle Tonio told Rosa, mi mestiza.

They flipped when she joined a chapter of La Raza Nueva. Dad railed: A terrorist organization! And us born in countries we've occupied! Amazed that Caltech even permitted LRN on campus. The family got visits from Homeland Security. Eggs and paint bombs from the neighbors. Caltech looked into it and found that of its seven members, five weren't students. LRN was a creation of Homeland Security. Rosa and Sean were the only two authentic members, and they kept bailing out of planned actions.

Her father came to her while Homeland Security was on top of them, in the dark of her bedroom. He sat on the edge of the bed, she could feel his weight there and the displacement of it, could smell faintly the alcohol on his breath. He said: My mother and my father, my sisters, after the invasion, we lived in cardboard refrigerator boxes in the median strip of the main road from the airport to the city. For a year.

He'd never told her that. She hated him. For sparing her that, only to use it on her now. She'd known he'd grown up poor, but not that. She said bitterly: Behind every fortune is a crime. What's yours?

He drew in his breath. She felt him recoil, the mattress shift under his weight. Then a greater shift, unfelt, of some dark energy, and he sighed. I won't deny it, but it was for family. For you! with sudden anger.

What did you do?

That I won't tell you. It's not safe.

Safe! You always want to be safe, when you should stand up!

Stand up? I did the hardest things possible for a man to do. For you, for this family. And now you put us all at risk—. His voice came close to breaking.

When he spoke again, there was no trace of anger left. You don't know how easily it can all be taken from you. What a luxury it is to stand up, as you call it.

Homeland Security backed off when Caltech raised a legal stink about entrapment. She felt vindicated. But her father didn't see it that way. *The dumb luck*, he called it, *of a small fish*. Stubborn in his way as she.

Sean, her lovely brother, who'd taken her side through all this, decided to stand up in his own perverse way: he joined the Army. She thought it was dumb, but she had to respect his argument: it was unjust that only poor Latinos joined. Certainly Papá, the patriot, couldn't argue with that logic, though he was furious.

Six months later Sean was killed in Bolivia. Mamá went into a prolonged, withdrawn mourning. Papá stifled an inchoate rage.

She'd met Roger Fry when he taught her senior course in particle physics; as "associated faculty" he became her thesis advisor. He looked as young as she. Actually, he was four years older. Women still weren't exactly welcome in high-energy physics. Rosa—not cute, not demure, not quiet—was even less so. Roger, however, didn't seem to see *her*. Gender and appearance seemed to make no impression at all on Roger.

He moved north mid-semester to work at the Lab but continued advising her via e-mail. In grad school she followed his name on papers, R.A. Fry, as it moved up from the tail of a list of some dozen names to the head of such lists. "Physics of milli-K Antiproton Confinement in an Improved Penning Trap." "Antiprotons as Drivers for Inertial Confinement Fusion." "Typical Number of Antiprotons Necessary for Fast Ignition in LiDT." "Antiproton-Catalyzed Microfusion." And finally, "Antimatter Induced Continuous Fusion Reactions and Thermonuclear Explosions."

Rosa applied to work at the Lab.

She didn't stop to think, then, why she did it. It was because Roger, of all the people she knew, appeared to have stood up and gone his own way and had arrived somewhere worth going.

• • •

They were supposed to have landed on the planet twelve years ago.

Nothing was out there in the dark. Nothing had followed. They were alone. That was worse.

She weighed herself. Four kilos. That would be forty in Earth gravity. Looked down at her arms, her legs, her slack breasts and belly. Skin gray and loose and wrinkled and hanging. On Earth she'd been chunky, glossy as an apple, never under sixty kilos. Her body had been taken from her, and this wasted, frail thing put in its place.

Turning on the monitor's camera she had another shock. She was older than her mother. When they'd left Earth, Mamá was fifty. Rosa was at least sixty, by the look of it. They weren't supposed to have aged. Not like this.

She breathed and told herself it was luxury to be alive.

• • •

Small parts of the core group met face to face on rare occasions. Never all at once—they were too dispersed for that and even with travel permits it was unwise—it was threes or fours or fives at most. There was no such thing as a secure location. They had to rely on the ubiquity of surveillance outrunning the ability to process it all.

The Berkeley marina was no more secure than anywhere else. Despite the city's Potemkin liberalism, you could count, if you were looking, at least ten cameras from every point within its boundaries, and take for granted there were many more, hidden or winged, small and quick as hummingbirds, with software to read your lips from a hundred yards, and up beyond the atmosphere satellites to read the book in your hand if the air was steady, denoise it if not, likewise take your body temperature. At the marina the strong onshore flow from the cold Pacific made certain of these feats more difficult, but the marina's main advantage was that it was still beautiful, protected by accumulated capital and privilege—though now the names on the yachts were mostly in hanzi characters—and near enough to places where many of them worked, yet within the tether of their freedom—so they came to this rendezvous as often as they dared.

I remember the old marina. See where University Avenue runs into the water? It was half a mile past that. At neap tide you sometimes see it surface. Plenty chop there when it's windy.

They debated what to call this mad thing. Names out of the history of the idea—starships that had been planned but never built—Orion, Prometheus, Daedalus, Icarus, Longshot, Medusa. Names out of their imagination: Persephone, Finnegan, Ephesus. But finally they came to call it—not yet the ship, but themselves, and their being together in it—Gypsy. It was a word rude and available and they took it. They were going wandering, without a land, orphaned and dispossessed, they were gypping the rubes, the hateful inhumane ones who owned everything and out of the devilry of ownership would destroy it rather than share it. She was okay with that taking, she was definitely gypsy.

She slept with Roger. She didn't love him, but she admired him as a fellow spirit. Admired his intellect and his commitment and his belief. Wanted to partake of him and share herself. The way he had worked on fusion, and solved it. And then, when it was taken from him, he found something else. Something mad, bold, bad, dangerous, inspiring.

Roger's voice in the dark: I thought it was the leaders, the nations, the corporations, the elites, who were out of touch, who didn't understand the gravity of our situation. I believed in the sincerity of their stupid denials—of global warming, of resource depletion, of nuclear proliferation, of population pressure. I thought them stupid. But if you judge them by their actions instead of their rhetoric, you can see that they understood it perfectly and accepted the gravity of it very early. They simply gave it up as unfixable. Concluded that law and democracy and civilization were hindrances to their continued power. Moved quite purposely and at speed toward this dire world they foresaw, a world in which, to have the amenities even of a middle-class life—things like clean water, food, shelter, energy, transportation, medical care—you would need the wealth of a prince. You would need legal and military force to keep desperate others from seizing it. Seeing that, they moved to amass such wealth for themselves as quickly and ruthlessly as possible, with the full understanding that it hastened the day they feared.

• • •

She sat at the desk with the monitors, reviewed the logs. Zia had been the last to waken. Four and a half years ago. Trouble with the magsail. It was gone, and their incoming velocity was too high. And they were very close now, following his trajectory to the B star. She looked at his calculations and thought that he'd done well; it might work. What she had to do: fine-tune the elements of the trajectory, deploy the sunshield, prime the fuel, and finally light the hydrogen torch that would push palely back against the fury of this sun. But not yet. She was too weak.

Zia was dead for sure, on his slab, shriveled like a nut in the bodysuit; he had gone back into hibernation but had not reattached his stents. The others didn't look good. Fang's log told that story, what she'd done to combat the fungus, what else might need to be done, what to look out for. Fang had done the best she could. Rosa, at least, was alive.

A surge of grief hit her suddenly, bewildered her. She hadn't realized it till now: she had a narrative about all this. She was going to a new world and she was going to bear children in it. That was never a narrative she thought was hers; hers was all about standing up for herself. But there it was, and as the possibility of it vanished, she felt its teeth. The woman she saw in the monitor-mirror was never going to have children. A further truth rushed upon her as implacable as the star ahead: the universe didn't have that narrative, or any narrative, and all of hers had been voided in its indifference. What loss she felt. And for what, a story? For something that never was?

• • •

Lying next to her in the dark, Roger said: I would never have children. I would never do that to another person.

You already have, Rosa poked him.
You know what I mean.
The universe is vast, Roger.
I know.
The universe of feeling is vast.
No children.
I could make you change your mind.

• • •

She'd left Roger behind on Earth. No regrets about that; clearly there was no place for another person on the inside of Roger's life.

The hydrogen in the tanks around the ship thawed as they drew near the sun. One tank read empty. She surmised from logs that it had been breached very early in the voyage. So they had to marshal fuel even more closely.

The ship's telescopes had been watching, and the computers processing, so the system's orbital elements had been refined since Zia first set up the parameters of his elegant cushion shot. It wasn't Rosa's field, but she had enough math and computer tools to handle it. Another adjustment would have to be made in a year when they neared the A star, but she'd point them as close as she could.

It was going to be a near thing. There was a demanding trade-off between decel and trajectory; they had to complete their braking turn pointed exactly at where A would be in a year. Too much or too little and they'd miss it; they didn't have enough fuel to make course corrections. She ran Zia's app over and over, timing the burn.

Occasionally she looked at the planet through the telescope. It was there. Still too far away to see much. It looked like a moon of Jupiter seen from Earth. Little more than a dot without color, hiding in the glare of A.

It took most of a week to prep the rocket. She triple-checked every step. It was supposed to be Sergei's job. Only Sergei was not on the ship. He'd left no log. She had no idea what had happened, but now it was her job to start up a twenty-gigawatt gas-core fission reactor. The reactor would irradiate and superheat their hydrogen fuel, which would exit the nozzle with a thrust of some two million newtons.

She fired the attitude thrusters to derotate the ship, fixing it in the shadow of the sunshield. As the spin stopped, so did gravity; she became weightless.

Over the next two days, the thermal sensors climbed steadily to 1000°C, 1200, 1500. Nothing within the ship changed. It remained dark and cool and silent and weightless. On the far side of the shield, twelve centimeters thick, megawatts of thermal energy pounded, but no more than a hundred watts reached the ship. They fell toward the star and she watched the outer temperature rise to 2000.

Now, as the ship made its closest approach, the rocket came on line. It was astounding. The force pulled her out of the chair, hard into the crawlspace beneath the bolted desk. Her legs were pinned by her sudden body weight, knees twisted in a bad way. The pain increased as g-forces grew. She reached backwards, up, away from this new gravity, which was orthogonal to the floor. She clutched the chair legs above her and pulled until her left foot was freed from her weight, and then fell back against the bay of the desk, curled in a fetal position, exhausted. A full g, she guessed. Which her body had not experienced for eighty-four years. It felt like much more. Her heart labored. It was hard to breathe. Idiot! Not to think of this. She clutched the chair by its legs. Trapped here, unable to move or see while the engine thundered.

She hoped it didn't matter. The ship would run at full reverse thrust for exactly the time needed to bend their trajectory toward the farther sun, its nuclear flame burning in front of them, a venomous, roiling torrent of plasma and neutrons spewing from the center of the torus, and all this fury not even a spark to show against the huge sun that smote their carbon shield with its avalanche of light. The ship vibrated continuously with the rocket's thunder. Periodic concussions from she knew not what shocked her.

Two hours passed. As they turned, attitude thrusters kept them in the shield's shadow. If the shield failed, there would be a quick hot end to a long cold voyage.

An alert whined. That meant shield temperature had passed 2500. She counted seconds. The hull boomed and she lost count and started again. When she reached a thousand she stopped and shut her eyes. Some time later the whining ceased. The concussions grew less frequent. The temperature was falling. They were around.

Another thirty minutes and the engines died. Their thunder and their weight abruptly shut off. She was afloat in silence. She trembled in her sweat. Her left foot throbbed.

They'd halved their speed. As they flew on, the sun's pull from behind would slow them more, taking away the acceleration it had added to their approach. That much would be regained as they fell toward the A star over the next year.

She slept in the weightlessness for several hours. At last she spun the ship back up to one tenth g and took stock. Even in the slight gravity her foot and ankle were painful. She might have broken bones. Nothing she could do about it.

Most of their fuel was spent. At least one of the hydrogen tanks had suffered boil-off. She was unwilling to calculate whether enough remained for the second maneuver. It wasn't her job. She was done. She wrote her log. The modified hibernation drugs were already in her system, prepping her for a final year of sleep she might not wake from. But what was the alternative?

It hit her then: eighty-four years had passed since she climbed aboard this ship. Mamá and Papá were dead. Roger too. Unless perhaps Roger had been wrong and the great genius of humanity was to evade the ruin it always seemed about to bring upon itself. Unless humanity had emerged into some unlikely golden age of peace, longevity, forgiveness. And they, these Gypsies and their certainty, were outcast from it. But that was another narrative, and she couldn't bring herself to believe it.

6.

They'd never debated what they'd do when they landed.

The ship would jettison everything that had equipped it for interstellar travel and aerobrake into orbit. That might take thirty or forty glancing passes through the atmosphere, to slow them enough for a final descent, while cameras surveyed for a landing site. Criteria, insofar as possible: easy terrain, temperate zone, near water, arable land.

It was fruitless to plan the details of in-situ resource use while the site was unknown. But it would have to be Earth-like because they didn't have resources for terraforming more than the immediate neighborhood. All told, there was fifty tons of stuff in the storage bay—prefab habitats made for Mars, solar panels, fuel cells, bacterial cultures, seed bank, 3D printers, genetic tools, nanotech, recyclers—all meant to jump-start a colony. There was enough food and water to support a crew of sixteen for six months. If they hadn't become self-sufficient by then, it was over.

They hadn't debated options because they weren't going to have any. This part of it—even assuming the planet were hospitable enough to let them set up in the first place—would be a lot harder than the voyage. It didn't bear discussion.

SOPHIE (2126)

Waking. Again? Trying to rise up out of that dream of sinking back into the dream of rising up out of the. Momma? All that okay.

Soph? Upsa daise. Пойдем. Allons.

Sergei?

She was sitting on the cold, hard deck, gasping for breath.

Good girl, Soph. Get up, sit to console, bring spectroscope online. What we got? Soph! Stay with!

She sat at the console. The screen showed dimly, through blurs and maculae that she couldn't blink away, a stranger's face: ruined, wrinkled, sagging, eyes milky, strands of lank white hair falling from a sored scalp. With swollen knuckles and gnarled fingers slow and painful under loose sheathes of skin, she explored hard lumps in the sinews of her neck, in her breasts, under her skeletal arms. It hurt to swallow. Or not to.

The antisenescents hadn't worked. They'd known this was possible. But she'd been twenty-five. Her body hadn't known. Now she was old, sick, and dying after unlived decades spent on a slab. Regret beyond despair whelmed her. Every possible future that might have been hers, good or ill, promised or compromised—all discarded the day they launched. Now she had to accept the choice that had cost her life. Not afraid of death, but sick at heart thinking of that life, hers, however desperate it might have been on Earth—any life—now unlivable.

She tried to read the logs. Files corrupted, many lost. Handwritten copies blurry in her sight. Her eyes weren't good enough for this. She shut them, thought, then went into the supply bay, rested there for a minute, pulled out a printer and scanner, rested again, connected them to the computer, brought up the proper software. That all took a few tiring hours. She napped. Woke and affixed the scanner to her face. Felt nothing as mild infrared swept her corneas and mapped their aberrations. The printer was already loaded with polycarbonate stock, and after a minute it began to hum.

She put her new glasses on, still warm. About the cataracts she could do nothing. But now she could read.

They had braked once, going around B. Rosa had executed the first part of the maneuver, following Zia's plan. His cushion shot. But their outgoing velocity was too fast.

Sergei continued talking in the background, on and on as he did, trying to get her attention. She felt annoyed with him, couldn't he see she was busy?

Look! Look for spectra.

She felt woozy, wandering. Planets did that. They wandered against the stars. How does a planet feel? Oh yes, she should look for a planet. That's where they were going.

Four. There were four planets. No, five—there was a sub-Mercury in close orbit around B. The other four orbited A. Three were too small, too close to the star, too hot. The fourth was Earth-like. It was in an orbit of 0.8 AU, eccentricity 0.05. Its mass was three quarters that of Earth. Its year was about 260 days. They were still 1.8 AU from it, on the far side of Alpha Centauri A. The spectroscope showed nitrogen, oxygen, argon, carbon dioxide, krypton, neon, helium, methane, hydrogen. And liquid water.

Liquid water. She tasted the phrase on her tongue like a prayer, a benediction.

It was there. It was real. Liquid water.

• • •

But then there were the others. Fourteen who could not be roused. Leaving only her and Sergei. And of course Sergei was not real.

So there was no point. The mission was over however you looked at it. She couldn't do it alone. Even if they reached the planet, even if she managed to aerobrake the ship and bring it down in one piece, they were done, because there was no more they.

The humane, the sensible thing to do now would be to let the ship fall into the approaching sun. Get it over quickly.

She didn't want to deal with this. It made her tired.

• • •

Two thirds of the way there's a chockstone, a large rock jammed in the crack, for protection before the hardest part. She grasps it, gets her breath, and pulls round it. The crux involves laybacking and right arm pulling. Her arm is too tired. Shaking and straining she fights it. She thinks of falling. That was bad, it meant her thoughts were wandering.

Some day you will die. Death will not wait. Only then will you realize you have not practiced well. Don't give up.

• • •

She awoke with a start. She realized they were closing on the sun at its speed, not hers. If she did nothing, that was a decision. And that was not her decision to make. All of them had committed to this line. Her datastream was still sending, whether anyone received it or not. She hadn't fallen on the mountain, and she wasn't going to fall into a sun now.

• • •

The planet was lost in the blaze of Alpha A. Two days away from that fire, and the hull temperature was climbing.

The A sun was hotter, more luminous, than B. It couldn't be approached as closely. There would be less decel.

This was not her expertise. But Zia and Rosa had left exhaustive notes, and Sophie's expertise was in winnowing and organizing and executing. She prepped the reactor. She adjusted their trajectory, angled the cushion shot just so.

Attitude thrusters halted the ship's rotation, turned it to rest in the sunshield's shadow. Gravity feathered away. She floated as they freefell into light.

Through the sunshield, through the layers of carbon, aerogel, through closed eyelids, radiance fills the ship with its pressure, suffusing all, dispelling the decades of cold, warming her feelings to this new planet given life by this sun; eyes closed, she sees it more clearly than Earth—rivers running, trees tossing in the wind, insects chirring in a meadow—all familiar but made strange by this deep, pervasive light. It might almost be Earth, but it's not. It's a new world.

Four million kilometers from the face of the sun. 2500°C. *Don't forget to strap in.* Thank you, Rosa.

At periapsis, the deepest point in the gravity well, the engine woke in thunder. The ship shuddered, its aged hull wailed and boomed. Propellant pushed hard against their momentum, against the ship's forward vector, its force multiplied by its fall into the star's gravity, slowing the ship, gradually turning it. After an hour, the engine sputtered and died, and they raced away from that radiance into the abiding cold and silence of space.

• • •

Oh, Sergei. Oh, no. Still too fast.

They were traveling at twice the escape velocity of the Alpha C system. Fuel gone, having rounded both suns, they will pass the planet and continue out of the system into interstellar space.

Maneuver to planet. Like Zia said. Take all genetic material, seeds, zygotes, heatshield payload and drop to surface, okay? Best we can do. Give life a chance.

No fuel, Sergei. Not a drop. We can't maneuver, you hear me?

Дерьмо.

Her mind is playing tricks. She has to concentrate. The planet is directly in front of them now, but still nine days away. Inexorable, it will move on in its orbit. Inexorable, the ship will follow its own divergent path. They will miss by 0.002 AU. Closer than the Moon to the Earth.

Coldly desperate, she remembered the attitude thrusters, fired them for ten minutes until all their hydrazine was exhausted. It made no difference.

She continued to collect data. Her datastream lived, a thousand bits per hour, her meager yet efficient engine of science pushing its mite of meaning back into the plaintext chaos of the universe, without acknowledgement.

The planet was drier than Earth, mostly rock with two large seas, colder, extensive polar caps. She radar-mapped the topography. The orbit was more eccentric than Earth's, so the caps must vary, and the seas they fed. A thirty-hour day. Two small moons, one with high albedo, the other dark.

• • •

What are they doing here? Have they thrown their lives away for nothing? Was it a great evil to have done this? Abandoned Earth?

But what were they to do? Like all of them, Roger was a problem solver, and the great problem on Earth, the problem of humanity, was unsolvable; it was out of control and beyond the reach of engineering. The problems of *Gypsy* were large but definable.

We were engineers. Of our own deaths. These were the deaths we wanted. Out here. Not among those wretched and unsanctified. We isolates.

• • •

She begins to compose a poem a day. Not by writing. She holds the words in her mind, reciting them over and over until the whole is fixed in memory. Then she writes it down. A simple discipline, to combat her mental wandering.

• • •

In the eye of the sun
what is not burned to ash?

In the spire of the wind
what is not scattered as dust?

Love? art?
body's rude health?
memory of its satisfactions?

Antaeus
lost strength
lifted from Earth

Reft from our gravity
we fail

Lime kept sailors hale
light of mind alone
with itself
is not enough

• • •

The telescope tracked the planet as they passed it by. Over roughly three hours it grew in size from about a degree to about two degrees, then dwindled again. She spent the time gazing at its features with fond attention, with longing and regret, as if it were the face of an unattainable loved one.

It's there, Sergei, it's real—Ghost Planet Hope—and it is beautiful—look, how blue the water—see the clouds—and the seacoast—there must be rain, and plants and animals happy for it—fish, and birds, maybe, and worms, turning the soil. Look at the mountains! Look at the snow on their peaks!

This was when the science pod should have been released, the large reflecting telescope ejected into planetary orbit to start its yearlong mission of measuring stellar distances. But that was in a divergent universe, one that each passing hour took her farther from.

We made it. No one will ever know, but we made it. We came so far. It was our only time to do it. No sooner, we hadn't developed the means. And if we'd waited any longer, the means would have killed us all. We came through a narrow window. Just a little too narrow.

She recorded their passing. She transmitted all their logs. Her recent poems. The story of their long dying. In four and a quarter years it would reach home. No telling if anyone would hear.

So long for us to evolve. So long to walk out of Africa and around the globe. So long to build a human world. So quick to ruin it. Is this, our doomed and final effort, no more than our grieving for Earth? Our mere mourning?

Every last bit of it was a long shot: their journey, humanity, life itself, the universe with its constants so finely tuned that planets, stars, or time itself, had come to be.

Fermi's question again: if life is commonplace in the universe, where is everyone? How come we haven't heard from anyone? What is the mean time between failures for civilizations?

Not long. Not long enough.

Now she slept. Language was not a tool used often enough even in sleep to lament its own passing. Other things lamented more. The brilliance turned to and turned away.

• • •

She remembers the garden behind the house. Her father grew corn—he was particular about the variety, complained how hard it was now to find Silver Queen, even the terminated variety—with beans interplanted, which climbed the cornstalks, and different varieties of tomato with basil inter-planted, and lettuces—he especially liked frisee. And in the flower beds alstroemeria, and wind lilies, and *Eschscholzia,* the California poppy. He taught her those names, and the names of Sierra flowers—taught her to learn names. We name things in order to love them, to remember them when they are absent. She recites the names of the fourteen dead with her, and weeps.

• • •

She'd been awake for over two weeks. The planet was far be-hind. The hibernation cocktail was completely flushed from her system. She wasn't going back to sleep.

• • •

ground
rose
sand

elixir
cave

root
dark

golden

sky-born

lift
earth
fall

• • •

The radio receiver chirps. She wakes, stares at it dumbly.

The signal is strong! Beamed directly at them. From Earth! Words form on the screen. She feels the words rather than reads them.

We turned it around. Everything is fixed. The bad years are behind us. We live. We know what you did, why you did it. We honor your bravery. We're sorry you're out there, sorry you had to do it, wish you . . . wish . . . wish . . . Good luck. Goodbye.

Where are her glasses? She needs to hear the words. She needs to hear a human voice, even synthetic. She taps the speaker.

The white noise of space. A blank screen.

• • •

She is in the Sierra, before the closure. Early July. Sun dapples the trail. Above the alpine meadow, in the shade, snow deepens, but it's packed and easy walking. She kicks steps into the steeper parts. She comes into a little flat just beginning to melt out, surrounded by snowy peaks, among white pine and red fir and mountain hemlock. Her young muscles are warm and supple and happy in their movements. The snowbound flat is still, yet humming with the undertone of life. A tiny mosquito lands on her forearm, casts its shadow, too young even to know to bite. She brushes it off, walks on, beyond the flat, into higher country.

• • •

thistle daisy cow-parsnip strawberry clover
mariposa-lily corn-lily ceanothus elderberry marigold
mimulus sunflower senecio goldenbush dandelion
mules-ear iris miners-lettuce sorrel clarkia
milkweed tiger-lily mallow veronica rue
nettle violet buttercup ivesia asphodel
ladyslipper larkspur pea bluebells onion
yarrow cinquefoil arnica pennyroyal fireweed
phlox monkshood foxglove vetch buckwheat
goldenrod groundsel valerian lovage columbine
stonecrop angelica rangers-buttons pussytoes everlasting
watercress rockcress groundsmoke solomons-seal bitterroot
liveforever lupine paintbrush blue-eyed-grass gentian
pussypaws butterballs campion primrose forget-me-not
saxifrage aster polemonium sedum rockfringe
sky-pilot shooting-star heather alpine-gold penstemon

• • •

Forget me not.

THE NINE BILLION NAMES OF GOD

Dear Mr. Scholz,

Regarding your submission, "The Nine Billion Names of God": I shouldn't even bother to respond, but I don't want you to think that I'm gullible. Plagiarism occurs in science fiction as elsewhere, but I've never before seen anyone submit a word-for-word copy of another story, let alone a story as well known as Arthur C. Clarke's "The Nine Billion Names of God." For you to imagine that any editor could fail to recognize this story implies a real ignorance of, and contempt for, our field. In the future I will not welcome your submissions.

Sincerely,
Robert Sales
Editor
NOVUS Science Fiction

Dear Mr. Sales,

Well, this is what comes of submitting without a cover letter. Of course I knew you would recognize Clarke's story, and I hoped that you would infer the reasoning behind my story, which I freely admit is word-for-word the same as Clarke's. Nonetheless, there are important differences, which I shall explain.

First, this story could not have been written today. Too much of the internal evidence is against it. If a reader recognizes the story, the clue is obvious, and the disorientation is instant. Otherwise, an uneasiness will grow at mention of the "Mark V computer" with its "thousands of calculations a second," the "electromatic typewriters," "Sam Jaffe," and other obvious anachronisms.

On top of this, I have avoided using the conventional meanings of words. For example, when I use "machine," I intend "a vast and barren expanse of land" or "an outmoded philosophical system." Naturally this presents difficulties. The invention (or redefinition) of words is nothing new to science fiction, but I doubt if it has ever been done on this scale, where every single word in a story has a meaning unique to that story. (The new meanings are all tabulated in a glossary that I chose not to submit, economy being the first virtue of art; a short story with explanatory notes the length of a novel would be ridiculous.)

So there is enough depth here to interest a reader. There is the "mask" of the Clarke narrative, behind which lurks my own narrative, told in my "invented" language, and behind that is the story of my story: how a contemporary work of prose came to resemble superficially a science fiction story of the 1950s. These are deep questions of context; as the identical arrangement of letters (such as *elf* or *pain)* may mean differently in different languages, so my arrangement of words "means" very differently than Clarke's.

There is more, but I think this sufficient for now. The story is difficult, I admit, but not inaccessible. I think your readers are intelligent enough to deal with it.

Of course, I understand your reluctance. After all, if I may say so, your publication has gained a certain reputation for stodginess, and your more conservative readers would probably find "The Nine Billion Names of God" too avant-garde.

Yours,
Carter Scholz

Dear Mr. Scholz,
Are you for real? Are you saying you've used the words of Clarke's story to stand in, one-for-one, for other words, like a cryptograph? It's absurd. I don't believe a word of it. Even the idea is derivative. I'm sure I've seen it in Borges. In its most basic form this notion of changing the context of an artifact might make a readable story, but certainly not this way.

There's no need to blame my "conservative" readers for the rejection. Just blame me.

Sincerely,
Robert Sales

Dear Mr. Sales,
Since you ask, here is the revised ms. As you can see, no words have been changed, but experience should teach you to look further. I have revised my glossary and appendices, and changed some rules of grammar, along with quite a lot of the history of the world from which this artifact purports to come. Also—a nice touch, I think—the articles in the story have all

been restored to their original meanings. "A" is "a," "the" is "the," etc.

There is so much information in the world already that I find it more revealing to create new contexts than new information. It would be more accurate to compare my work to Warhol or Duchamp than Clarke or Borges, whom in any case I have not read.

Sincerely,
Carter Scholz

Dear Mr. Scholz,
Incredible. I had no idea you would resubmit "your" story—with "revisions," no less! I am re-returning it. I don't want to see it again, ever. I don't care if it's "really" derivative of Duchamp or Warhol or Gustave Flaubert. Just leave me alone.
RS

Dear Mr. Sales,
This time I'm lowering my sights a little. I think you'll find this story really funny. It's a kind of "parody-by-repetition." This kind of parody is effective with works of a "baroque" nature, that is, works based on the logical, exhaustive permutations of a few principles. Science fiction stories are "baroque" because they are the intellectual children of empiricism, so they tend to offer explanations, and they tend to exhaust a limited repertoire of materials. The ambition of explanations is to be complete, so such systems tend to be closed, and this closure leads naturally to repetition and counterfeiting, endlessly evident in rack after rack of books about plucky young wizards or wisecracking star-ship tailgunners. The sportive élan of early

science fiction has spiraled into an abortive ennui, and its writers face an endgame situation, in which the remaining moves are few and predictable. Clarke's monks naming the names of God from AAAAAAAAA to ZZZZZZZZZ (with the help of a computer) no more surely faced the end of their world. My "counterfeit" of Clarke is more interesting, more purely "speculative" than this other sort of plagiarism. Here, the very act of quoting becomes parody, much like the act of moving a soup can from the supermarket to a gallery. It makes ridiculous the soup, the gallery, the audience, and the artist. It unites them.

Sincerely,
Carter Scholz

PS. There are several refinements in this draft. I hope you don't think I'm overworking it. Since each time I submit it its context is changed, of course you are not really seeing the "same" "story" "again." There are no "agains" in this game.

Dear Mr. Scholz,
No! I see no changes in the story, but you are definitely overworking me!

You seem to have a good mind. Why not do something constructive with your time? Save yourself postage and save me grief.

Yours, again, still, and for the last time,
Bob Sales

"Dear" "Mr." "Sales,"
A "text" "admits of" numerous "interpretations." The "interpretations" "become" more "numerous" as "time" "passes."

Most "important," "it" seems to "me," is the "act" of "reprinting" "The Nine Billion Names of God" "today." "Presenting" it in that "context" "sets up" a "series" of "speculations" more "interesting" than those "raised" by most of the "stories" "you" "publish." This "matter" of "context" is a kind of "Last Question" for "art," "literature," and "ultimately" "science fiction." The "real" "story" always "lies" "outside" the "words"—in "context," "implication," and "association"—in what is "not" "written." "Surely" "you" can "see" "that"? Let "us" be "brave," and "pursue" the "implications" of "our" "activities."

"Sincerely,"
"Carter Scholz"

Dear Mr. Scholz,
How would it be if I bought the story and didn't publish it? Would that get you off my back? The quotes in your last letter gave me eyestrain, and I'm beginning to dread opening my mail.

Yours,
Sales

Dear Mr. Sales,
Since I am obviously among friends, since you understand that words mean only what we are conditioned to think they mean (legitimated in dictionaries according to the biases of lexicographers), I will dispense with the quotes. And I will tell you something that I previously withheld. My story, "The Nine Billion Names of God," was generated by a computer. But let me approach this new development by stages.

Like any number of people (your mailbox must be jammed with their efforts), I once thought I would like to write science fiction. For several years I worked at it, until the notion had passed from a hobby to an avocation to a passion to an obsession. Never has so much energy been turned to such small account. I failed, utterly, exhaustively, repeatedly; daily, yearly, by degrees and in large lots, I failed. I collected a tower of rejections informing me it had all been done better, and probably with less effort, by Clifford Simak or Curt Siodmak in 1947. And in truth, looking over my millions of failed words, I could no longer tell whether they were very much better, very much worse, or about the same as the published works I had set out to emulate.

By now I was not in my right mind. Have you ever lain awake at night, repeating a simple word like "clown" over and over, until it loses its meaning? Entire stories reached that insane pitch for me. In my sleep I would get rejection letters about my own dreams. Only a long course of therapy brought me back to a point where I could, more or less, construct sentences.

So I gave it up and went back to school.

My graduate studies were about randomness. In one course I made a random number program to simulate the motion of gas molecules in a closed space. By varying the "temperature" of the space I could control the degree of randomness. I used the numbers to select words from a dictionary, and generate random texts; late at night I found their incoherence soothing. But one night, in the midst of this placid gibberish, the machine suddenly gave out the complete text of "The Nine Billion Names of God."

As in cliché fiction, the hackles did stand on my neck. I printed the pages. I checked the network in vain for any sign of a prankster.

I shut down the machine and went home. There I compared my printout to the published Clarke text. Word for word it was the same. There was nothing strange about it, except for where and how it had appeared. After a few stiff drinks, I began to feel lighthearted. For there it was, at last, the product of my labors, a vindication, a light at the end of a closed universe, the annihilisation of the etym, the big bang. I had produced a real science fiction story, and a certified classic at that! However obliquely, I had become a science fiction writer; I had, in fact, with exactly the same words, achieved more subtlety, depth, and irony than Clarke himself. How could I doubt it? For, unlike Clarke's story, mine could be verified at the atomic level.

Well, I thought to give myself the Fields Prize for math and a Nebula Award for best story. In a fever I devised my histories, glossaries, and so on, as I have previously explained. I created a unique context for an extant text, a story as commonplace in the world of science fiction as Campbell's soup is to *tout le monde*.

Running the program backwards, by the way, produced Asimov's "The Last Question."

But this brings me to the central problem. If gas molecules (or their stand-ins), capering at random, can produce a pattern equivalent to the pattern of words in "The Nine Billion Names of God," or "The Last Question," or indeed in time any text, even those not yet written—then why write? An author publishes from doubt, I think; he wants the world to regard him as real, substantial, genuine. But in this case, does such confirmation matter? Can one persuade molecules?

The pattern of any story can be found in the random phenomena of nature. The air hums. Daily the ten thousand things recite all nine billion names. A rainstorm, a gust of wind, the bending of a tree, heat waves, all are instinct with a wisdom beyond signs, more engaging than any story because they encompass and can engender all stories. You may find a story in a tree, but never a tree in a story, only the constellation of letters *tree,* and the crushed remains of one in the paper. Why tell stories if all the stories that ever could be are told constantly in the wind and the rain? That is the real last question: Do we need fiction? Do we need science?

I labored years with my ambition, and have learned that it is pointless. The end of ambition is to end ambition, just as the point of a fiction is to subsume lesser fictions, and the end point of all fiction is to reach that supreme fiction, the world. Though not without a journey.

But we have taken that journey before. In our stories we have gone past Mercury and Pluto; inclined in worshipful orbit to our great gods Speed and Death, those creators and annihilators of meaning, we have turned a thousand times in a thousand tales. We have seen the engines of our imagination actually built and lifted into space, and they have not meliorated our plight. I think we may never reach a plain sense of things as long as we have either science or fiction to hide behind.

The story of the story of my story ends here. Believing this, I must withdraw my manuscript from submission. I hope you understand. I'd rather not see any more stories published anywhere.

Thank you for your interest.

Sincerely,
Carter Scholz

Dear Contributor:

We are returning your manuscript because publication of *NOVUS Science Fiction* has been discontinued. Thank you for your interest.

The Editor

THE UNITED STATES OF IMPUNITY

THE NEW CENTURY HAS been kind to nothing lawful. It really got going with the Supreme Court's appointment of Bush, which Gore could have legally challenged but did not. But even before that in California we had a foretaste of what things were going to be like. We had an "energy crisis." Starting in the summer of 2000, reaching crisis level in 2001, public utilities suddenly faced up to fortyfold increases in their supply prices.

Why were power utilities paying for power? Because deregulation, signed into law by Governor Pete Wilson in 1996, had put the utilities' generating plants into the hands of private, unregulated, out-of-state companies such as Duke, Mirant, Reliant, Williams, Dynergy, El Paso, and Enron. The new owners ran schemes that took generators offline at peak hours for unneeded "maintenance," manipulated power grids and natural gas pipelines, and otherwise gamed the so-called free market. The utilities themselves, called the Investor Owned Utilities—such a cute acronym—were left holding the bag. They couldn't raise their rates because their rates *were* regulated. So a state of emergency was declared by our incumbent governor, the hapless Gray Davis. To keep the lights on, California was forced to enter into extortionate long-term contracts, which cost the state's taxpayers, in the long run, at least $30 billion. In November 2003, a recall election stripped Davis of office and replaced him with Arnold Schwarzenegger.

The Federal Energy Regulatory Commission, which is mandated to ensure "just and reasonable" rates, issued a statement that the inflated rates were "not just or reasonable," yet they failed to intervene or censure any of the players. Vice President Cheney's "Energy Task Force," convened in secret in February 2001, released no minutes and did nothing about the California crisis.

It should be unnecessary to say this: critical social infrastructure, on which lives depend, should not be run for unregulated profit, because this "market" is captive, and the consequences of bad behavior are too ruinous for society to tolerate. The safe areas should include utilities, health care, insurance, courts, prisons, public safety, education, defense, intelligence, transportation, communications, and banks. Instead, almost every one of these areas has seen in recent years a full-court press to put these public goods into private hands.

Enron collapsed—though not because of its role in defrauding California—and its CEO and CFO were prosecuted, as were some other fraudsters in the telecom industry at about that time. But it's the job of pioneers to take arrows; lessons were learned, and much larger frauds lay ahead, for which no one would be held accountable.

• • •

The financial crisis of 2008 had a precursor in the savings and loan crisis of the 1980s. It's instructive to compare the fallout of the two events.

In the '80s, the total amount of money lost was $400 billion; it cost the United States $160 billion. One thousand FBI agents commenced over five thousand criminal investigations. There were one thousand convictions. That many S&L officials went to jail.

Estimates of the cost to the public of the 2008 crisis range from $6 to $40 trillion. Nobody seems to know for sure, but it looks to be about fifteen to a hundred times as large. Convictions: one. That would be Lorraine O. Brown, president of a company that produced fake mortgage documents for banks. The banks that ordered up the fake documents— Bank of America, Chase, Wells Fargo, Citi, GMAC—cut a deal and paid a "cost of doing business" fine.

The credit rating agencies Moody's and Standard & Poor abetted the fraud by giving AAA ratings to the banks' securitized sacks of shit. Unlike the accounting firm Arthur Andersen, which had to surrender its license after lying for Enron, there were no consequences for the agencies.

Only the public lost money. The Treasury printed trillions of dollars under the rubric of "quantitative easing" and essentially gave it to the banks. Merrill Lynch, having lost $27 billion in 2008, took $10 billion from the Fed and handed out $3.6 billion of it immediately in bonuses to executives. The Fed dropped interest rates to zero, where they remain seven years later, effectively stealing from anyone prudent enough to have savings.

It's tempting to blame Republicans for 2001–2008, but this friendliness to chicanery is thoroughly bipartisan. It was the Gramm-Leach-Bliley Act, signed into law by Clinton in 1999, that repealed the Glass-Steagal Act, removing the barriers between investment banking, commercial banking, and insurance, thus directly enabling the 2008 crisis. Glass-Steagal, passed in 1933 to curb the banking excesses that caused the Great Depression, had been under attack by the financial industry ever since, but it took the direct efforts of men like Robert Rubin and Lawrence Summers, Clinton's Treasury secretaries, to finally kill it. It was Obama who appointed Summers his top advisor on managing the crisis Summers had done so much to enable. It was Obama's Justice Department under Eric Holder that declined to prosecute any executives involved in the criminality that triggered the collapse. A lone wolf like Bernie Madoff, who stole from elites, went to jail; those with systemic ties, who stole from the public, didn't.

• • •

Another relevant precursor to 2008 was the bailing out of the hedge fund Long Term Capital Management in 1998. The fund engaged in a highly specialized form of arbitrage bond-trading involving minute differences in interest rates. To be profitable, these trades had to be large, thus highly leveraged. The principals in the firm (including two Nobel Prize winners in economics for work on "risk management") were convinced that their mathematical models eliminated all risk from the scheme. For a few years the strategy worked. But in 1998, when Russia defaulted on its bonds, the wheels came off. The company had $4 billion in capital, but through its exceptional leverage was exposed to a trillion dollars in losses. These losses threatened to bring down fifty other firms. The Federal Reserve Bank of New York stepped in to arrange a bailout, an unheard-of intervention at that time. Fourteen banks ponied up to keep the hedge fund going long enough for an orderly shutdown. In this case the partners were the big losers, not the public, but it was still an egregious instance of "moral hazard"—of pushing the costs of a risk onto other parties.

One of the lessons allegedly learned, according to a report issued by Merrill Lynch, one of the bailers, was that mathematical risk models "may provide a greater sense of security than warranted; therefore, reliance on these models should be limited." But the same defective risk models, and the same insane degree of leverage, caused the 2008 crisis. (As Peter Cook says in the "Frog and Peach" routine, "I've learned from my mistakes, and I can repeat them exactly.") After the 1998 blow-up, the LTCM principals went on to head up other hedge funds, using more or less the same strategy. One now advises pension funds.

Never mind that the models were defective. (Nassim Taleb is especially pungent on their elementary statistical misconceptions.) Even bankers have the right to be venal and stupid. But not the right to push the costs of their mistakes onto others.

The belief that risk can be managed leads to riskier behavior. Either it provides a false sense of security, or less innocently it enables fraud by shifting the risk to a counterparty. By the rationality of the market, when looting has no risk, it's irrational *not* to loot.

The "risk management" instruments at the heart of the 2008 meltdown—credit default swaps, collateralized debt obligations, securitized mortgages—had exactly the opposite effect of their stated goal of reducing risk. In this they were like "enhanced interrogation" or drone warfare, which respectively promise truthful information and precisely targeted killing, and provide the opposite.

• • •

The urge to put public funds into private pockets also has pervaded, one might almost say driven, our foreign policy. We subcontracted huge parts of the Iraq war to private contractors. At times they outnumbered the troops. It was far more costly to hire Halliburton (later called KBR) to provide the construction, sanitation, food, and security services that once were provided by rear-echelon soldiers, but it had two advantages: it avoided a draft and it distributed huge sums with little or no accountability. The contracts were no-bid and cost-plus. That is, they guaranteed a profit over reported costs, whatever those might be. KBR made at least $40 billion. With no competition, KBR never had to provide cost estimates, or proof of costs; they simply handed in bills. When army auditors questioned the lack of documentation, KBR had the auditors fired. They made employees sign confidentiality agreements that in effect made it illegal to report fraud. Ninety percent of their invoices were never audited.

In 2003 the United States also shipped to Iraq $15 or $20 billion—no one seems to know exactly how much—in shrink-wrapped blocks of hundred-dollar bills. Many billions of it—again, no one knows how much, perhaps as much as $13 billion—simply disappeared. It was "walking-around money" for the use of viceroy Paul Bremer's Coalition Provisional Authority. No one seemed to mind that the money itself got up and walked away.

Consider Cheney's cavalier response to the looting of Iraq's National Museum of priceless Sumerian artifacts: "Stuff happens." Over 80 percent of the museum's holdings were looted while US troops stood by and watched.

The "stuff" that has happened most since 2001 is just this kind of breathtakingly rapid, shameless, felonious plundering of trillions of dollars. Military subcontracting, education, emergency management, homeland security, private prisons, and health insurance have all proved rich troves of public money for the taking. The wholesale privatization of public functions, begun in earnest in 1981 when Ronald Reagan broke up the air traffic controllers' union, has moved into the most central functions of government.

There was far greater criminality in Iraq than theft and fraud. There was the torture of prisoners at Abu Ghraib and elsewhere. There was the repeated killing of civilians. In every case only a few low-level actors were held accountable while the architects of the policies that created the criminogenic situations went untouched.

First and foremost was the invasion itself. When UN inspectors were on the verge of concluding that Iraq possessed no weapons of mass destruction and, contrary to the Bush administration's claims, posed no threat to the United States or any other nation, the United States attacked anyway. That decision had been taken before the inspections started.

"To initiate a war of aggression, therefore, is not only an international crime; it is the supreme international crime differing only from other war crimes in that it contains within itself the accumulated evil of the whole." That is Supreme Court Justice Robert H. Jackson in 1946, writing as chief of counsel for the United States at Nuremberg. Fifty-seven years later, the United States had evidently changed its mind, for under international law, which the United States had done so much to advance at Nuremberg, the only justifications for waging war are self-defense, treaty obligations, or a UN resolution. None of these applied to Iraq.

Reporters like Judith Miller, who "catapulted the propaganda" for the war, were rewarded. Miller eventually and rightly lost her job at the *New York Times* in 2005 over the inaccuracy of her prewar reporting, but she still works as a journalist, and also for the Manhattan Institute and the Council on Foreign Relations. As recently as April 2015 she published a book-length self-serving account of her faulty *Times* reporting in the *Wall Street Journal*. Reporters like Robert Scheer, who wrote in opposition to the war at the *LA Times*, were fired.

The architects and the boosters of this catastrophic war, the longest and most costly in US history, which achieved nothing but the destruction of Iraq, were not chastened, but have continued to espouse the same preemptive belligerence toward Libya, Syria, Iran, and Ukraine. As Taleb said mildly of one of the LTCM principals, after errors of such magnitude all of these people "should be in a retirement home doing Sudoku," not holding forth on Sunday talk shows and sitting on think tanks and advising 2016 presidential candidates. Many should be on trial for war crimes.

Yet after the Democrats won both houses of Congress in 2006, and all this was abundantly clear, Speaker of the House Nancy Pelosi announced, "Impeachment is off the table." Pelosi's oath of office requires her to defend and protect the U.S. Constitution. Clear and plausible evidence existed that the Bush administration had committed high crimes and misdemeanors, by lying to Congress and the American people and by starting an illegal war of aggression against Iraq. Pelosi had no right or power to take impeachment "off the table"; indeed, she had the unmistakable duty to initiate articles of impeachment. So did every other member of Congress, but as Speaker she bears particular responsibility for this grant of impunity.

Even before Iraq, the creation of the Guantánamo prison camp, and the treatment of detainees there—and in Bagram, and at an unknown number of other "black sites"—were also international crimes, yet to be charged or prosecuted. The lawlessness of these sites has two dimensions: the prisoners, contrary to jurisprudence since the Magna Carta, are held indefinitely and without charges, and abused in clear and documented violation of national and international statutes, while their captors escape accountability for these criminal violations.

Candidate Obama said he would close Guantánamo; but as to justice, even before his inauguration he said, "Look forward, not back," and those responsible for instigating, justifying, and maintaining the torture regime, as well as the illegal war, were let walk. This normalized and made bipartisan the most extreme abuses of the Bush years. In some cases Obama extended the abuses: he has prosecuted and jailed whistleblowers under the egregious 1917 Espionage Act, and he continues to use "state secrets" privilege to dismiss without a hearing lawsuits brought by victims of this system. This posture led ACLU president Anthony Romero to propose in a 2014 op-ed that Obama should pardon all the offenders, because at least that would suggest that something had occurred that needed pardoning. (I made the same proposal in early 2009 in a mood of bitter irony, but Romero was serious.)

• • •

Our national security apparatus was likewise largely subcontracted to private parties. In 2004 alone, $42 billion in contracts were handed out. The boondoggles and abuses are too numerous to catalog, but let's look at the most criminal: the National Security Agency's mass surveillance of Americans.

The details are now well known, but it's another sign of bipartisanship that the NSA abuses had at least one predecessor. Since at least 1992 the Drug Enforcement Agency has been bulk-collecting billions of telephone call logs—every single call made from the United States to a "drug-trafficking country" (more than a hundred countries in all)—under a program authorized successively by Bush Senior, Clinton, Bush Junior, and Obama. It was halted only in late 2013, after Edward Snowden's revelations brought home to the DOJ that it might be pushing its luck to keep a second illegal surveillance program running.

The impunity with which the DEA violated the law for twenty-one years was an inspiration and a model for the NSA. However enthusiastically the Bush administration embraced the model, it wasn't their invention.

All these abuses were bipartisan. The Senate Intelligence Committee was fully briefed on torture and on warrantless wiretapping. Pelosi's reluctance to impeach was rooted in her complicity. Senator Ron Wyden repeatedly warned of these surveillance excesses, although in vague terms. He lacked the courage to reveal the classified details on the Senate floor, even though the Constitution gives him the immunity to do so.

An earlier attempt at the universal surveillance state was the 1994 campaign for the Clipper Clip. This encryption technology was to be embedded in every cell phone as a way of "securing" communications. The algorithm had been developed by the NSA, was secret, and had a back door for law enforcement access. The campaign for its adoption was spearheaded by Vice President Gore. Resistance from the computer community stopped it.

We should be so lucky today. When the scale of the NSA's warrantless wiretapping was revealed, the Democratic-controlled Congress passed a law in 2008 to grant retroactive immunity to the telecoms that complied with NSA's lawless requests. The immunity granted was so comprehensive that it even kept the public from learning just what the telecoms had done. Candidate Obama swore at first to oppose the bill, but he voted for it. The media were likewise complicit when it counted. *New York Times* executive editor Bill Keller delayed James Risen and Eric Lichtblau's reporting on warrantless wiretapping for over a year at the request of the White House, until after the 2004 election.

•••

Impunity and kleptocracy feed one another. Ideology and profit coevolve. They provide cover for each other. Profiteers fund ideologues, and ideologues provide legitimation to profiteers. The "free market" is the favored ideology in the United States, and its reach keeps extending.

The NAFTA free-trade agreement—unsuccessfully pushed by Reagan and Bush, finally secured by Clinton in 1994—proved to be disastrous for all but the transnational corporations that sponsored it. Coming trade agreements will be far worse. Congress just gave Obama fast-track authority for the Trans-Pacific Partnership, with two similar agreements waiting in the wings. The TPP alone covers 40 percent of the world economy. The text of the agreement is actually *classified*—only a few select Congressmen are permitted to read sections of it under highly restrictive conditions. WikiLeaks and the *New York Times* published one chapter of it. That chapter describes its "investor-state dispute settlement" mechanism. Investors may challenge regulations, laws, and government actions—federal, state, and local—before private tribunals. If a tribunal rules that some local statute—an environmental regulation, say—poses a risk to an investor's *expected future* profits, it can award damages in unlimited amounts. The three-person tribunals are made up of lawyers unaccountable to any electorate or legal system. The lawyers rotate between acting as judges, and representing investors in cases against governments; there are no conflict of interest rules. There is no appeal or review mechanism.

It's easy to imagine an insurance company feeling its future profits threatened by a nation's move to enact single-payer health care, or an oil company deciding that profits are being lost to a carbon tax. Even the threat of a large settlement might chill legislation or regulation. In one case brought under earlier agreements, Occidental Petroleum was awarded $2 billion from the republic of Ecuador. The Swedish nuclear firm Vattenfall is suing Germany for $4 billion over Germany's decision to shut down nuclear power plants.

This represents the global expansion of a supranational extralegal regime. It guarantees investors' profits at public expense. It aims to grant ultimate sovereignty to the corporation as the supreme form of social organization.

• • •

The real costs of this endemic impunity lies ahead. By declaring some banks "too big to fail," thus implicitly guaranteeing bailouts, the United States and Europe guarantee a recurrence of 2008. By legitimizing the use of rendition and torture, by disdaining *habeas corpus*, the United States in effect licenses other powers to do the same and loses any moral authority to protest human rights abuses by others. By waging "preventive" war against Iraq, it has shown by example that this is acceptable. During the Cold War, the relative parity of force, and the unspeakable consequences—the "balance of terror"— restrained the Soviet Union and the United States. Smaller powers, with or without nuclear weapons, might not be so restrained. And the cost to the global standing and influence of the United States from its recent excesses of force and impunity is most likely to be paid by further force and impunity. This posture is not sustainable, but as long as there is no direct cost to policy-making elites, it will stand.

The greatest cost, to all, is the direct misery that issues from the use of force, and the attendant destruction of ethical norms. When a crime leaves no legal trace, wrongdoing is normalized. There is no societal record, no judgment, no consensus memory of it. Wrongness then has no cause, no human agency; it just happens. This sort of lie eats away at a cooperative social fabric. Like Iraq's looted antiquities, relics of civilization and legality vanish from a shared heritage into private vaults, there to be brandished only as trophies and weapons—an insult and a menace to every community and every individual who ever worked to set human relations on grounds other than force and coercion.

BAD PENNIES

TESTIMONY of Deputy Director RICHARD SNOW

Thank you, sir. It's a pleasure to be here again.

I first met Mr. Kak in—wait, is, is the date classified? Let's just say in the nineteen eighties. He came to my attention, to the Agency's attention, through a series of memos from the station chief in Vinograd, where Mr. Kak lived at the time.

The Vinograd regime was unresponsive to diplomacy. The Agency wanted to inject $1 billion in colorable local currency into the black market, thus destabilizing the—yes, Senator?

Colorable. We don't use the word "counterfeit."

Well, Senator, there is ample precedent. I mean, the Brits did it to the Soviets, the Germans did it to the Brits, the Paks did it to the Indians. In Vietnam the United States issued what we call parody currency, solely as a propaganda front.

The actual manufacture of the currency? I can't discuss that.

Okay. We set up a firm in Vinograd, called Polemonium Assets, with Mr. Kak in charge. He made loans, he procured infrastructure from local businessmen, et cetera. But despite a massive injection of really very well made banknotes, the official economy stayed flat. There was no price inflation, no rush to redeem old bonds, no pressure on the central bank or the government. Because the General ordered the central bank: As long as no one withdraws, there's no problem.

Okay, so with the official currency sequestered, our notes were traded on the street. And there was a general upturn. Goods and services returned to Vinograd. Houses were painted, flowers appeared in windowboxes. There was a, wait, sorry, here it is, a wary cheerfulness, as one of our assets put it. People were happier. The General took note of this, and he took credit. He was photographed in a street market eating an orange.

What? No, sir. I believe it was simply that the General thought the image resonated with a populace long deprived of oranges, and he wished to associate himself with the, the sudden orange, so to speak.

Okay, so contrary to our intents, there was no inflation, no pressure on the government. Then Mr. Kak suggested to the central bank that they establish a secondary market in our colorables. Brilliant idea. Pretty soon they were trading above the genuines. With its newfound liquidity, the central bank issued a series of high-yield bonds, and foreign investors snapped them up. Mr. Kak's firm saw large profits.

Yes, I mean no. Mr. Kak's accounting practices in this period weren't quite up to American standards. I don't think we can determine now exactly where every penny went.

Well, Senator, it seems to me there's a double standard here. I mean, first of all, yes it's a striking irony, if you want to put it that way, that Polemonium Assets actually propped up the government we meant to overthrow but after all, Senator, by the time the central bank defaulted it was Citibank not Polemonium propping them up, and you're not going after Citibank, are you?

In the first six months alone Mr. Kak's company created a half billion dollars in new wealth not to mention—yes, Senator?

The cost? You mean of producing the currency or, of, of the whole project?

Around $3 billion.

Yes, but Senator, we started with counterfeits, and the wealth Mr. Kak created was real. He took a fictitious wealth and he, he, ah, bonified it. That is entrepreneurism, Senator. I don't think you want to disparage that.

Okay, our original goal was to bring down the economy, yes. But that was only a tactic in the service of regime change. In the long run we achieved our goal, once the General closed the central bank and fled with the assets.

The bank's assets then were about $4 billion. At that juncture Mr. Kak closed the doors of his company as well.

Well, sir, that is a matter for the international banking community to resolve. We did not permit the General to skip town, as you put it, nor did we have orders to stop him. If the European and American banks that invested have a problem, I think they can solve it in the usual way.

"Bailout" isn't the word I'd use. To me this is a matter of protecting an investment in democracy.

Democracy, sir, is when people get to choose a government that gives them freedom in the marketplace. But to return to the other gentleman's question, banks make loans all the time, all over the world; why is this different? There's risk in any enterprise—

Senator, I disagree.

That is a regrettable choice of words, Senator.

No, sir, Mr. Kak was not and is not an Agency asset, certainly not. He is, he was always, that is, he was an independent contractor. He never drew a salary.

No, sir, the General was never an asset. I don't know where you got—

That would fall under protecting sources and methods.

On behalf of the former Secretary, I object. There was no indictment.

Yes, thank you. I would, I would like to get back on track if the gentleman will let me. At that point, after the collapse of the government, Polemonium Assets was acquired by a startup called Peregrine Capital in McLean, Virginia.

I'm pleased to hear your concern and the committee's concern on this issue. Okay, briefly. The Agency does have a vital ongoing interest in the sort of situations that may threaten the United States. We would like to be in a position to encourage what you might call preventative diplomatic economic efforts. Mr. Kak proved an acute observer and a nimble mover in this arena. That was our purpose in helping Peregrine Capital set up shop in the United States. Peregrine provided us insight and clarity concerning world market forces. That's all.

Yes, Mr. Kak took on partners at that time.

Yes, the former Secretary was one.

I guess you'd call it a hedge fund. The prospectus says, wait, Peregrine Capital seeks out arbitrage opportunities in international currency markets.

Peregrine did very well in its first two years, posting re-turn to investors of about 40 percent per annum. This gave Peregrine very good standing with creditor banks. They lever-aged about $10 billion of invested capital into positions of about a half trillion dollars.

Yes, sir, trillion.

May I continue? It wasn't all roses. When the Thai baht collapsed, Peregrine lost quite a lot. A lot of investors did. Japanese banks were perhaps the hardest hit.

Mr. Chairman, thank you for pointing that out. It's as you say a sort of silver lining that more favorable US trade balances with Asia resulted.

What? Senator, I don't know where you got that but—

Well, *Financial Times* or not I think—manipulating the baht—sweeping in with his associates to buy valuable state assets at knockdown prices—I mean, that's not a fair assess-ment. That doesn't square with the facts on the ground. The market is what it is. You can accept that or you can try to turn back the tide.

Yes, thank you, Mr. Chairman, I'm sure we don't want to, to get into the macro, I mean the micro, I mean I'm not a financial expert. My concern is with the national security implications.

The next summer, Russia defaulted on its international loans, leading to more losses for Peregrine. At that point the Federal Reserve became worried about the effect on world markets if the hedge fund failed, so the Fed arranged a recapi-talization of Peregrine through a consortium of private banks. Peregrine's holdings at that point were about one point $5 trillion. Their capital was down to about three billion. That's, what is that, fifty to one?

Okay, five hundred to one leverage.

Moral hazard? I don't understand the term.

Sir, Alan Greenspan said it was not a bailout. Can we move on?

Part of the recap deal was that Mr. Kak stay on as manager for a year. At the same time, Mr. Kak established the Palladium Group. It, wait, the prospectus says it offers high level strategic advisory and advocacy services to international clients and to government agencies.

No, the Agency has no connection with Palladium.

I'm not familiar with those names.

It is possible that some retired Agency personnel are employed by Palladium. We don't tell our retirees what to do.

Sir? I don't know what you're inferring.

Again, Senator, there were no convictions in that matter, and I wonder why you keep digging up ancient history.

Okay, that, yes, that recent operation got a lot of, of press, didn't it? Yes, by all means, let's talk about that operation. That operation had both military benefits and security benefits and economic benefits. First, the contraband fissile material was interdicted at the border. Second, the quantity was relatively small. Third, it proves that market forces treat this kind of contraband material the same as any other material. To me, that says the operation was a success. It creates an opportunity for us. As a result of it, we have a new tool for fighting terrorism.

Yes, exactly, Mr. Chairman. A sting. First we sell it to them and then we take it back. This creates a market for the material, which drives up the price, which forces terror groups to spend themselves into a downward spiral. Since we're a market-maker in this material, other players will come to us and that also gives us a chance to repatriate some of the contraband material that's got out there over the years.

Uh, how much, how much contraband material is out there—isn't that classified?

No? Okay, if you insist, about twelve thousand kilograms. That we know of. More or less.

A, a weapon? You mean a device. You could make a nuclear device from, ah, about six kilograms of this material.

I think that would make twenty? Two hundred? No, okay, two thousand devices. More or less.

Mr. Chairman, again, I want to come back and say I'm pleased to hear your concern and the committee's concern on this issue. I have to go and refresh myself on this, but I don't think—I think that if it's a trade issue—I mean, is it fair trade practice to take in fissile material and introduce it to the market without having any cost associated? We'll have to study that, sir.

No, Senator. I don't think this is a matter of where Mr. Kak is or isn't or what he has or hasn't done. It's more about the roles we have established for the kinds of players that best fill them.

You've already heard testimony from the Vice President and from the gentlemen at Treasury, Justice, and State on how valuable Mr. Kak has been to them. In closing let me say that he is a patriot twice over. He has served and sacrificed for his homeland, and for his adopted country. He has served on advisory panels, he has testified before Congress on several occasions, and there should be no further delay in confirming his appointment as our next Secretary of Homeland Security.

Yes, sir. Nice to see you too. Thank you. You make me blush.

"GEAR. FOOD. ROCKS."
Carter Scholz interviewed by Terry Bisson

On the cover of this book you appear to be heading out into the Universe on foot. Are those clip-art stars or an actual destination? Won't you need more than two poles and a daypack to get there?

The star field is the sky surrounding Alpha Centauri as seen from Earth. You can read *Gypsy* to learn just how much more you'd need to get there, but the ultralight principles are shared. That pack holds everything I need for seven days out.

What drew you into (or toward) science fiction? What was your first sale?

My family was profoundly unliterary. I remember a short shelf of Reader's Digest Condensed Books, my father's engineering texts, my mother's Gregg shorthand manuals, and that was it. So in adolescence I read my way, with the indelible joy of escape, through our public library's science fiction shelves. Afterward, I found further indelibility: Eliot, Beckett, Kafka, Faulkner, Joyce, Pound. I was drawn to the core modernist works, not so much to the Updike and Cheever domestic realism that was dominant at the time, despite my living in the landscape it described. What it said wasn't true to my experience in 1960s suburban New Jersey. Science fiction seemed the nearest extant thing to modernism, and to my experience.

My first sale was an accident. I attended the 1973 Clarion SF Workshop, and my characteristic, class-traitor response to that was to write a long, non-SF "mainstream" story about the last NASA Apollo mission titled "The Eve of the Last Apollo." Kate Wilhelm, one of my instructors at Clarion, had asked me to send her a story for a forthcoming workshop anthology, so I sent this, with a cover letter apologizing for its inappropriateness. She passed it, literally, across the kitchen table to her husband, Damon Knight, and he said, so he told me, "It's mine!" He published it in his legendary hardcover anthology *Orbit*, even though it wasn't SF by any definition but his. All us young'uns who knew them then owe Damon and Kate: they spent a lot of publishing capital helping us unknowns.

You have been published both in and out of the science fiction category. Was this by design or chance? Do you consider genre a help or a hindrance to the serious writer?

I think a serious writer largely ignores category and genre when at work. Category is what your publisher calls you, and where you get shelved in the bookstore. Genre is more complicated; that involves the whole history of your reading, your affinities, and so it implicates category as well. But yourself and your idea of literature is always bigger than that.

I submitted my novel *Radiance* to Bryan Cholfin, then an editor at Tor, a science fiction publisher, because he'd been kind enough to buy a couple of stories from me for his magazine *Crank*. Bryan literally walked across the hall from Tor to PicadorUSA, both owned by St. Martins, subsidiaries of Macmillan, then owned by Bertelsmann—I don't know the current Borg masters. Bryan did me a noble, spirited service by his walk, and he'll always be my friend for that, though it did neither of us any negotiable good. Genre depends a great deal on your point of view.

I wrote an essay many years ago that claimed Beckett's *The Lost Ones* as SF, and Gaddis's *JR*, also most of Calvino and Pynchon and Borges (whose first publication in North America, I note with genre satisfaction, was in the pages of *Fantasy and Science Fiction*, then edited by Anthony Boucher). I don't mean to appropriate them into our category, but to proclaim that this mode of "imaginative" storytelling, rather than the strictly "realistic," has been with us far longer and is more fundamental.

Gypsy is what we in SF call a "starship novel." You didn't invent the form. Do you recall when you first encountered it?

As a teenager in that public library. Probably "Far Centaurus" by A.E. van Vogt. In van Vogt's story, the first starship is so long in its traveling that a newer faster-than-light ship is invented and overtakes it and has a colony up and running before the slow ship arrives.

I've never seen an SF story take full stock of how hard, maybe impossible, interstellar travel is going to be. *Gypsy* is my attempt to do it "with the net up," as the "hard SF" writers say. Even in the most rigorous hard SF, you always reach the hand-wave moment where the net drops to permit some bit of story development. I wanted to play it straight and let the story come out of the constraints of the physics. Even the made-up parts, such as the ship's fusion engine, aren't my invention. I drew all the extrapolated technologies from published research papers and hewed to their limits. I'm not a physicist, but I grew up and was educated during the Cold War, when math and science education were priorities, so I understood enough to be able to run gravity simulators on my computer to model the Alpha C system, spreadsheets to model various flight times, et cetera. All the mechanics of the journey—all the moving parts, the times and trajectories—are as accurate as I could make them, physically and astronomically.

So I've come full circle. My first published story was a mainstream story about a returned astronaut in the 1970s alienated by his experience from domestic "realism." This story is truly hard SF, the first I've ever written, with physically realistic constraints on what can happen.

You have also written for music magazines. Did you like the Beach Boys? Do you now?

I wrote for music technology magazines, such as *Keyboard* (thanks, Dominic Milano), which is not the same thing at all. The question should be, "Did you like MIDI?" Who are the Beach Boys?

You also play jazz piano, are an accomplished if amateur astrono-mer, and make pretty good wine. What's your best guess of a thread that unites these talents?

Attention deficit disorder?

What's a gamelan? Do they get good mileage?

Gamelan is the orchestra and the music of Indonesia, which is a made-up state comprising many cultures, each with its own distinct music. I first heard Balinese gamelan on a Nonesuch Explorer album, those glories of the 1970s, but I ended up playing for many years the very different Javanese form under the tutelage of Pak Cokro, Midiyanto, Jody Diamond, and Ben Brinner. Considering the average distance my teachers covered from Yogyakarta and Surakarta to Berkeley and back over all those years, I'd say the mileage is considerable. Pak Cokro's own mileage is even better: he has a recording on *Voyager*, currently twenty billion kilometers out and counting.

Ever miss New York? What brought you to the Bay Area? What keeps you here?

Sure I miss it, but the New York I grew up in has forever passed for me. My last visit was in 2010, when my younger stepdaugh-ter looked at colleges. It seemed like aliens had taken over mid-town. As a kid I used to ride the elevator up to the observation deck of the Empire State Building fairly often—a couple of times per year. I think it cost a quarter. When Amalie and I went up, as I'd promised her, the tab was somewhere north of a hundred bucks for us both. The Whitney and the MOMA are now displaced, and my beloved Hayden Planetarium has been replaced by something created by consultants. My Soho, in the late 1970s, centered on Sam Rivers's and Rashied Ali's jazz lofts, and that locale and scene is so gone it's not even lamentable.

I had friends in Berkeley, and I came for a visit in late 1977. I decided to stay on January 1, 1978. It was a gorgeous day, 70 degrees, and I was driving with a friend on Highway 1 in Sonoma County. We stopped to eat some lunch overlooking the ocean up on a two-hundred-foot cliff. My mind was already blown. Then a pod of whales breached below us. I knew I was staying.

What keeps me here is the sheer physical beauty of the place. We're so blessed that the California Coastal Commission (thank you, Jerry Brown), the East Bay Regional Park District, and the East Bay Municipal Utilities District have secured so much open space in and around our urban sprawl. Above all, the Sierra Nevada keeps me here.

What do you and Kim Stanley Robinson talk about when you're tramping about in the Sierras?

Weather. Wildlife. Gear. Food. Rocks. Route. Proust.

What was the origin of your novel about the Livermore Labs, Radiance? *Have you ever worked in high tech?*

For a time I did a little technical writing and coding for some very low-tech outfits, but my primary sources are credited in the acknowledgments: Andrew Lichterman and Daniel Marcus. Andy ran lawsuits against the Lab, and Dan worked there, so I had access to fairly intimate knowledge of the place from two very different perspectives. But the origin was simply living in the Bay Area. You couldn't not be aware of the Lab, especially during the SDI period, which *Radiance* covers. I consider it primarily about the California landscape, physical and psychic.

You seem equally adventurous in music and literature. At least in SF and jazz. Do you find the balance between pattern and innovation, expectation and surprise, similar in both or different?

Very similar. SF and jazz, these days, are generally not all that adventurous. They're mostly (not entirely) in archival mode, reliving and remixing past glories. And what glories. Both SF and jazz had a great run in New York City in the 1950s. The number of SF magazines and the number of jazz clubs, combined with the affordability then of life in the city, enabled a good number of really fine artists to make a living without a day job, to play every night or publish every month, enough to make a real scene.

The scenes crossed others as well, such as the avant-garde. Horace Gold, the editor of *Galaxy* magazine, hosted John Cage and Morton Feldman in poker games at his home in Peter Cooper Village, where I grew up. Orrin Keepnews—the Riverside Records producer who did so much for the careers of Bill Evans, Thelonious Monk, and so many others—started out as a book editor at Simon and Schuster and worked on several early SF hardcover titles. Culture is a wild seed, so who knows, but I see some of the '60s born in this cross-fertilization.

This year, 2015, is the fiftieth anniversary of the AACM (Association for the Advancement of Creative Musicians), born in Chicago. Check them out.

You and Jonathan Lethem authored a book together. What was that process?

When Jonathan lived in Oakland, he and I had often had lunch together. One day he showed me a notebook entry that in its entirety read "KAFKA / CAPRA." He said, "I think there's a story there." I went home and thought about it and wrote a thousand words about an emigré Kafka in '30s Hollywood. We passed it back and forth. In the course of this collaboration, we found that we'd each previously written a story involving Kafka. If we'd each write one more, he suggested, we'd have a slender book. Jonathan's energy turned this frail beginning into a real book, first from Subterranean Press (thank you, Bill Schafer), then from Norton (thank you, Aimee Bianca).

One of James Baldwin's favorite novels was The Princess Casamassima. *Did you know that?*

No.

Jeopardy answer (you provide the question): The Rapture of the New.

What is this morning?

You write as well as play music. How does musical composition differ from literary? Procedurally, I mean.

When you play, that is, improvise, which is composing in real time, you don't get the liberty of afterthoughts and fixing mistakes. But procedurally I think both kinds of composition start with improvisation, on some theme that's maybe a little vague at first, which gains more definition and direction the more you work on it. As a "composer" of music, you're doing this out of real time, which can be a benefit or a disadvantage. As a writer of prose, you're way better off hiding from real time.

What kind of car do you drive? (I ask this of everyone.)

A 1995 Honda Civic CX. It was stolen a few years ago. I learned from the internet that it was, at that time, the most stolen automobile in the USA—that year and model. It's easy to break into. The internet says you can open it with a tennis ball: make a slit in the ball, hold it against the door lock, squeeze it just right, and the air pressure holds back the tumblers. Nice going, Honda. Still, a great car. I got mine back and hope to keep driving it till I'm too old to care. Its appearance already shows that.

Do you listen to music when you write?

Never. Too distracting.

What are you reading this week? Next week?

This week, the scurrilous verse of John Wilmot, earl of Rochester. Next week, I wish I knew. (That's the title of a song by Harry Warren.)

Why do drivers take so long to get moving when the light changes?

Idiocracy.

Each in one sentence, please: James Salter, Don Pullen, Cecelia Holland, Antoni Gaudí.

Outsiders all; all underappreciated, except for Gaudí. I'm going to cheat with semicolons.

Salter wrote like some kind of tortured but undisgraced angel; he hid his Jewishness, and his angelic writing was always in some fear or disdain of its god Hemingway, but his integrity was his own.

Also his disappointment.

My first piano heroes are Monk and Evans, but Pullen could play anything—jazz, gospel, Afro-Brazilian, and, most powerfully, free.

Cecelia Holland can write about any period as if she'd lived her whole life in it, coming away with a fine understanding of how individual wills and a cultural moment create very particular moral complexities; if she'd written only three or four such novels that would be impressive, but she's written thirty or forty, which inspires awe.

I haven't ever stood within Gaudí's architecture, but the photos I've seen are stunning and remind me of standing within Simon Rodia's Watts Towers, and of the work of the German painter Hundertwasser, both I believe inspired by him, and both underappreciated.

Favorite Shakespeare play?

Tamburlaine Part 3. But it was actually written by Francis Bacon.

You are a charter member of a legendary San Francisco writers' workshop that almost never meets. Is that a problem or a strategy?

We consider it both. We're meeting "soon." That's the title of an underappreciated Gershwin tune.

BIBLIOGRAPHY

Novels

Palimpsests (1984) with Glenn Harcourt
Radiance (2002)

Collections

Cuts (1985)
Kafka Americana (1999) with Jonathan Lethem
The Amount to Carry (2003)

Short fiction

"The Eve of the Last Apollo" (1976)
"Closed Circuit" (1977)
"The Ninth Symphony of Ludwig van Beethoven and Other
        Lost Songs" (1977)
"Travels" (1980)
"Amadeus" (1980)

"The Johann Sebastian Bach Memorial Barbecue and
        Nervous Breakdown" (1980)
"In Reticulum" (1981)
"The Last Concert of Pierre Valdemar" (1981) also appeared
        as "s=1/2at2" (1981)
"Altamira" (1981)
"At the Shore" (1984)
"Intrusions" (1984)
"The Menagerie of Babel" (1984)
"A Catastrophe Machine" (1984)
"The Nine Billion Names of God" (1984)
"A Grim Tale for Moderns" (1985)
"Cuts" (1985)
"How Should We Celebrate the Bicentennial" (1985)
"Lineage" (1985)
"Players, or Some Problems of Form in New York" (1985)
"Recursion" (1985)
"The Sickness" (1985)
"The Sky in Winter" (1985)
"Why We Have Technology" (1985)
"The High Purpose" (1985) with Barry N. Malzberg
"Galileo Complains" (1986)
"A Draft of Canto CI" (1986)
"Transients" (1988)
"Blumfeld, an Elderly Bachelor" (1993)
"Thus, to the Stars" (1994) with Barry N. Malzberg
"Receding Horizon" (1995) with Jonathan Lethem
"Radiance" (1995)
"Make It New" (1996)
"Mengele's Jew" (1996)

"The Amount to Carry" (1998)
"The Doctrine of Color" (2000) with Kathe Koja
"Invisible Ink" (2003)
"I Didn't Know What Time It Was" (2005)
"Bad Pennies" (2009)
"Clod, Pebble" (2010) with Kathe Koja
"Rim" (2010)
"Signs of Life" (2011)

Poems

"In the blue house" (1985)

Compositions

8 Pieces (2000)

Essays

"Inside the Ghetto, and Out" (1985)
"Introduction (Cuts)" (1985)
"Dance of Shadows" (1995)
"The Amount to Carry" (introduction) (2011)

ABOUT THE AUTHOR

Born in New York City and educated on the East Coast, Carter Scholz made his way to California in the 1970s and never looked back. He is a classically trained composer, a working bebop pianist (The Inside Men), and a deep-sky astronomer as well as a celebrated author of speculative fiction. In addition to literary SF, his work includes a "New Twilight Zone" episode for television, a "computer music" CD (*8 Pieces*) for Frog Peak Music, and an astronomical commentary on the work of Kenneth Rexroth.

He lives in the Berkeley hills, with sojourns in the high passes of the Sierra Nevada.

Available from the PM Press
Spectacular Fiction Series

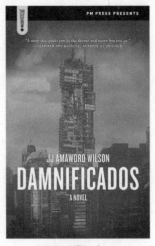

Damnificados
978-1-62963-117-2
$15.95

Clandestine Occupations
978-1-62963-121-9
$16.95

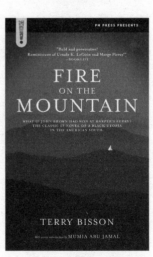

Fire on the Mountain
978-1-60486-087-0
$15.95

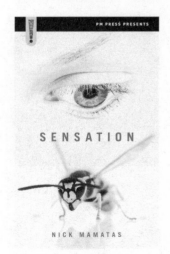

Sensation
978-1-60486-354-3
$14.95

Available from the PM Press
Outspoken Author Series

Report from Planet Midnight
978-1-60486-497-7
$12.00

The Great Big Beautiful Tomorrow
978-1-60486-404-5
$12.00

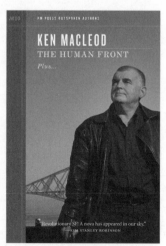

The Human Front
978-1-60486-395-6
$12.00

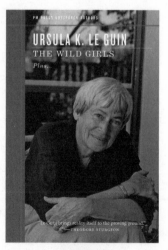

The Wild Girls
978-1-60486-403-8
$12.00

FRIENDS OF

PM

These are indisputably momentous times—the financial system is melting down globally and the Empire is stumbling. Now more than ever there is a vital need for radical ideas.

In the eight years since its founding—and on a mere shoestring—PM Press has risen to the formidable challenge of publishing and distributing knowledge and entertainment for the struggles ahead. With hundreds of releases to date, we have published an impressive and stimulating array of literature, art, music, politics, and culture. Using every available medium, we've succeeded in connecting those hungry for ideas and information to those putting them into practice.

Friends of PM allows you to directly help impact, amplify, and revitalize the discourse and actions of radical writers, filmmakers, and artists. It provides us with a stable foundation from which we can build upon our early successes and provides a much-needed subsidy for the materials that can't necessarily pay their own way. You can help make that happen—and receive every new title automatically delivered to your door once a month—by joining as a Friend of PM Press. And, we'll throw in a free T-shirt when you sign up.

Here are your options:
- $30 a month: Get all books and pamphlets plus 50% discount on all webstore purchases
- $40 a month: Get all PM Press releases (including CDs and DVDs) plus 50% discount on all webstore purchases
- $100 a month: Superstar—Everything plus PM merchandise, free downloads, and 50% discount on all webstore purchases

For those who can't afford $30 or more a month, we're introducing Sustainer Rates at $15, $10, and $5. Sustainers get a free PM Press T-shirt and a 50% discount on all purchases from our website.

Your Visa or Mastercard will be billed once a month, until you tell us to stop. Or until our efforts succeed in bringing the revolution around. Or the financial meltdown of Capital makes plastic redundant. Whichever comes first.

PM Press was founded at the end of 2007 by a small collection of folks with decades of publishing, media, and organizing experience. PM Press co-conspirators have published and distributed hundreds of books, pamphlets, CDs, and DVDs. Members of PM have founded enduring book fairs, spearheaded victorious tenant organizing campaigns, and worked closely with bookstores, academic conferences, and even rock bands to deliver political and challenging ideas to all walks of life. We're old enough to know what we're doing and young enough to know what's at stake.

We seek to create radical and stimulating fiction and non-fiction books, pamphlets, T-shirts, visual and audio materials to entertain, educate, and inspire you. We aim to distribute these through every available channel with every available technology—whether that means you are seeing anarchist classics at our bookfair stalls; reading our latest vegan cookbook at the café; downloading geeky fiction e-books; or digging new music and timely videos from our website.

PM Press is always on the lookout for talented and skilled volunteers, artists, activists, and writers to work with. If you have a great idea for a project or can contribute in some way, please get in touch.

PM Press
PO Box 23912
Oakland CA 94623
510-658-3906
www.pmpress.org

31901059491649